Shield

L.A. Storm 3

RJ Scott

V.L. Locey

Love Lane Books

Copyright

Shield (L.A. Storm, 3)

Copyright © 2024 RJ Scott, Copyright © 2024 V.L. Locey

Cover design by Meredith Russell, Edited by Sue Laybourn

Published by Love Lane Books Limited

ISBN - 9781785644740

All Rights Reserved

Shield

Can Jackson ensure the safety of his loved ones when the darkest elements of LA's underbelly seek retribution?

Oliver knows the clock is ticking on his dream of winning the Stanley Cup. After fourteen years playing for New York, he's beyond frustrated to leave friends behind when traded to the LA Storm. As a widower and father of two girls, he's facing the twilight of his career, and, worst of all, he's lonely. Making friends is easy enough, but he craves someone to hold him at night. When Jackson, equal parts grumpy chaos and charm, lands in his life, friendship turns to lust, and love isn't far behind. He finds himself drawn to Jackson, and as their relationship deepens, they become each other's haven amidst the chaos of their lives. However, danger from Jackson's work threatens their peaceful world, challenging their relationship and forcing love to take a backseat to survival.

After bringing down a notable money launderer, Jackson's small team receives orders to delve deeper into the world of organized crime in Hollywood. His early success quickly spirals into an overwhelming web of criminal intrigue. In this new, uncharted territory, he feels increasingly isolated, both personally and professionally. The more issues he uncovers, the less he seems to close. Meeting Oliver shakes his world even more, especially when he accidentally falls for the widower and father of two little girls. A few nights of fun is one thing, but deeper feelings and kids are something he is not at all prepared for. Yet, despite his reluctance, he becomes deeply attached to the little family who has embraced him with so much love. Now, he just has to shield them from the dangers that have followed him to their doorstep.

This opposites attract romance features a single dad hockey player grappling with personal loss, a grumpy detective entangled in the complexities of organized crime, and a love story that happens despite the odds.

Dedication

To my family who accepts me and all my foibles and quirks. Even the plastic banana in my holster.
VL Locey

Always for my family.
RJ Scott

L.A. STORM #3

SHIELD

RJ SCOTT & V.L. LOCEY

Love Lane Books

Chapter One

Oliver

THE ECHO OF PUCKS SLAMMING AGAINST THE BOARDS punched through the chilly arena air. I was already feeling the strain of practice as I glanced at my watch to check my sugar levels.

Lance "Ash" Ashman, my defensive partner, glided over with a youthful energy I envied. "Sugars okay?" he asked.

I nodded. Diabetes didn't define me, and it certainly didn't stop me from playing the game I loved, but fuck, it got in the way sometimes. It wasn't an impending hypo that made my legs feel like jelly. It was the fact that at thirty-five, every stride on the ice reminded me I was getting closer to the end of my career, and I wasn't a kid anymore.

"Yep," I said.

It was all Ash needed to know. The entire team had been subjected to a three-hour lecture by our team medic on the ups and downs of diabetes, and what to look out for, which meant that, for the next two practices, all of them stared at me, watching for me to appear drunk. I'd shut that down faster than a slapshot—they didn't need to stare —because I had alarms on alarms, a watch that connected to a sensor measuring my levels, and I wouldn't collapse in front of them.

Ash now had a permanent supply of candy in his cubby after taking things way too seriously. I could handle that, after all, he was my D-partner, but the fuss, I hated.

"Just not used to practices with just me and a couple of others."

"They don't do this shit in New York?"

I side-eyed him. "We're all there. I mean, we were all there, just separated off."

"You worried about facing the old team when it comes to it?" he asked, bouncing on his skates as we waited for the next attack.

"Nah," I lied.

Early next month, we'd be up against them, and despite the countless games under my belt—all sixteen years with the guys in the Big Apple—a knot of nerves settled in my stomach whenever I thought about it. It would be my first game against my old team since the trade, in the city itself, part of a larger East Coast stand that saw the LA Storm heading to Harrisburg and Boston as well, and it was a homecoming I wasn't sure I was ready for. Not only was it back there, against a team I'd grown up in, but I'd miss my girls like a limb.

Being traded hadn't been a surprise—deep down, I had seen the writing on the wall. At thirty-five, whispers of "*past his prime*" following my every move on the ice sparked fear. I knew hockey was a business. I understood the nature of the game, the inevitable cycle of players being traded, retiring, or being let go. But understanding it didn't make the reality any easier to stomach. New York had probably gifted me an extra year because of my situation, a widower balancing a demanding career with the needs of my daughters.

But New York had been my home, my team, my family. I'd given everything to the game, to the team, even when it meant juggling childcare for Scarlett and Daisy on my own after my wife had died. Losing Melissa to breast cancer had thrown our world into chaos, and I'd barely made it through intact, and only for my girls. The trade, though expected, stung with a bitterness that New York thought I wasn't useful anymore and had become a liability, rather than an asset.

So yeah, I was worried about fitting into the Storm's structure, and one day having to face my old team.

What if I fuck up?

My pride wanted to prove to the Storm that I still had value, that I wasn't just a player to be traded away when it was convenient as New York had done. Yet, there was also fear—the fear of not living up to my own expectations, of confirming the decision New York had made to let me go had been the right one.

The Storm had welcomed me with open arms, suggesting they wanted the experience and leadership I brought to the table. I was determined not to let them—or myself—down, and to show everyone I was more than the sum of my years. The fire of competition still burned bright.

And all I needed to do was fix the slow parts of my

game, keep up with the young guys, be the brick wall they needed me to be, and not fall over because my legs gave out.

Easy.

"Ready to take on Captain Fantastic?" Ash quipped, nodding toward Charles Zhang, Storm captain and first-line center, who was already weaving through cones with a puck at a mesmerizing pace. "*Practice with Cap*," Coach had said. "*If you can stop him, you can stop anyone*," he'd added, but fuck, Zhang was fast, and deadly accurate.

Still, I couldn't help but crack a smile. "Let's not let him dazzle us too much. Remember, we're supposed to be the wall, not the welcome mat."

Ash laughed, bumping his shoulder against mine before we both turned our attention to the task at hand. Philippe, our goalie, was bracing himself in the net, and I knew his focus would be sharp as Charles prepared to bear down on us.

The drill was simple—he was trying to get past us to score.

So simple.

Ash and I had to work seamlessly to stop him.

Yep. Simple.

Charles darted towards us, the puck glued to his stick. Ash and I moved in sync, a dance we'd been perfecting since I'd joined the team. Our aim was clear—keep Charles from finding even a sliver of space to break through or get a shot off. As our cap approached, I could see the determination in his eyes.

"Not today, Cowboy," he taunted, a grin spreading across his face as he attempted a feint to the left.

6

I didn't bite, staying square to him, my gaze locked on the puck. "In your dreams, Cap," I retorted, the familiar banter easing some of my tension.

He shifted direction, a quick movement meant to throw us off. But Ash was on him, forcing Charles to the outside. I closed the gap, ensuring there was no lane for a pass or shot, our sticks creating a barrier he couldn't penetrate.

"Nice try!" Ash shouted, a mix of challenge and respect in his voice as we steered Cap away from the net, the puck skittering harmlessly to the corner.

Philippe tapped his stick against the post, a sign of appreciation for the defensive effort. "Ha ha!" he shouted and patted his pipes, snickering as Cap skated around the back of the net. His grin widened when Cap collected the loose puck and attempted a baseball-type hit to get past our goalie. The two of them collapsed in a tangle of arms and legs, both laughing, and I took the moment to catch my breath.

"Water!" Ash announced, and as we skated back to the bench for a quick water break, he nudged me. "Hey, you've been pretty quiet about this New York game. You know we're gonna smash 'em, right?"

I hesitated. The weight of returning to a city that had been my home for so long was heavy on my shoulders. "It's not about winning; I know we're gonna win," I lied, because New York was a strong team. "It's just... y'know..." I didn't know how to explain.

As usual, Ash went all thoughtful and summarized everything in a sentence. The same skill at judging people on ice slid into real life all too easily. "You gave a lot to that team, to that city. And now, going back, not as one of them—it's a lot to process. But hell, it's gonna be a big party, you up on the video screen, crowds cheering." He raised his stick in a fake celebration and made a noise like a roaring crowd. "They're gonna love having you back, man. You're a legend there."

I felt hot, my heart twisting. I missed New York— moving across the country with the girls, being so far away from my best friend, Jamie, missing the guys on my old team—sometimes it was all too much like hard work.

Maybe I should just give up?

Why am I doing this?

What? Where had that hit of melancholy come from?

As if I'd already answered that question, my alarm sounded, and I glanced at my readings, popping a couple of Skittles from the supply I kept on the bench. The sugar was exquisite on my tongue, and I skated away from Ash, grinning at him as Cap circled us with a puck.

"Again?" I said, and even though I caught Cap and Ash exchanging thoughtful looks, neither one of them asked me if I was okay. "Let's go again."

"We're done, big guy," Cap murmured, elbowing me in the side.

"I'm good," I said, but Ash was already leaving the ice, which left me with the captain.

"The Nighthawks lost a good one," he said as we circled the rink, cooling down in lazy circles.

"You think?" Great, that sounded as if I was fishing for compliments.

"Oh yeah, don't you?"

We reached the door from the practice ice. "Yep." I

didn't talk much, but these one-word answers were even getting on my nerves.

"You're Storm now. We have you, and we're not letting you go."

I iced to a stop, waving Cap through first. His confidence was infectious, and I nodded along, the ongoing nerves slowly being replaced by a burgeoning sense of determination.

"Until I fuck up," I muttered to myself, because in the end, it wasn't about proving them wrong; it was about proving to myself that I still belonged in this game, age be damned.

As I revved the engine of my Ducati, pulling away from the practice arena, a sense of freedom washed over me. This bike was the only non-essential item I'd insisted on transferring to LA, and while my sensible SUV sat parked at home ready for the dad bits of my life, the Ducati was my one nod to being something other than a hockey player, widower, and father. An efficient way of navigating New York, it was just as handy in LA, and every time I rode her, I felt free of everything. Grief, cancer, losing Melissa, worrying about my kids, being a widower, starting over, they became somehow manageable as soon as I opened the throttle.

Not that there was a lot of fast riding on open roads—I was way too sensible to court danger at speed. Scarlett and Daisy had already lost their mom, and there was no way they were losing me if I could help it.

I'd promised Melissa.

With a couple of hours of free time before I needed to switch back into dad mode and pick up the girls from school, I headed to a place that had quietly become a significant part of my life here in LA, despite me having been in the city for only six weeks. Tucked away in the heart of Highland Park, a neighborhood far removed from the glitzy facade of Hollywood, stood the Haven of Hope Clinic. This place, a lifeline for the community, thrived on charitable donations, providing medical care and support to those in need.

The area around the clinic was a big contrast to the more affluent parts of LA I'd come to know. Still, Highland Park, with its aging buildings and signs of crime, had an authenticity and vibrancy that resonated with me. Despite its rough edges, there was life here, a community spirit the polished streets of Hollywood could never replicate.

I parked my Ducati in a small lot next to the clinic, the familiar sounds of the neighborhood enveloping me as I dismounted. The laughter of children as they played on the sidewalks, the distant buzz of traffic, and the occasional shouts from windows were more real to me than the place I'd grown up in the affluent Dallas suburbs where money was king. I could do some good here.

As I walked into the clinic, I immediately felt at home. There was a warmth and bustle to the place, volunteers chatting, trying to make a difference, kids crying, parents in groups. I waved to Lazlo at reception. He'd changed the color of his hair again—now blue from green—and he grinned at me.

"Yo, Cowboy," he called.

I headed that way. "Hey, Lazlo, is Joe in?"

Lazlo frowned, leaned closer, and lowered his voice. "He's gone all do-not-disturb, not seeing patients, and he's losing his shit with everyone who knocks on his door."

That didn't sound good. Joe was former military, a medic, and the guy who ran this place on nothing but fluff and buttons. He was ruthless at recruiting volunteers doctors and nurses, and an expert at guilting big pharma to donate. He might be rough and ready, but he was dragging this entire community to good health one case at a time. But he was also a gentle giant, loved people as much as they loved him, and losing his shit didn't sound like him at all. Maybe it was a money thing? I could help with that. I saved money every year for my girls, a trust fund that would see them happy and settled with a good start, but after that and my sole luxury—the Ducati—everything else I gave away.

Not that anyone knew, and they never would.

"Had a couple of referrals for you," Lazlo said, slapping some files down. "Why don't you take a coffee and see if you can cheer Joe up before you read them?"

Referrals were about moms with breast cancer—the same cruel disease that had taken Melissa—or those newly diagnosed with diabetes. In fact, any families who struggled where Lazlo thought I could help. I picked up the files, headed through the door to the consultation rooms, passing walls adorned with handmade posters and kids' art, and finally, through the last door, marked *staff only*, with my key card.

I knocked on the door, juggling paperwork and the

coffee, using my elbow on the handle, and tumbling inside with a grin on my face, all ready to cheer Mr. Grumpy up.

Only to find him at the wrong end of a gun, bleeding from a head wound and barely able to move.

The man with the gun—skinny and scarred—pointed the weapon at me, gestured for me to come in, the door closing behind me, then waved the gun at the other chair in the room. My gaze flew to the small, but bright yellow, smiley face on the back of the hand holding the pistol.

I tried to put my hands up, but I had the coffee and files. "Hey, whatever this is—"

"You! Shut the fuck up," the man snapped, then waved the gun wildly before turning it on Joe, who paled. "Get the fucking codes!" the man snarled, then left the room, leaving behind the smell of smoke and body odor.

I immediately went to Joe as he slid sideways out of the chair, catching him before he fell, blood smearing the desk and down my shirt. He was unconscious, and I couldn't think what to do.

The coffee had spilled, the files landed in a heap on the floor, and I yanked out my cell and called 911.

What the hell?

Chapter Two

Jackson

"… THEN SHE STARTED ASKING ME ABOUT MY PILES. I mean, who rightfully asks their son-in-law such a personal question? Do I ask her about her varicose veins?"

"God, I hope not," I replied as I stared into the vast emptiness of an empty Minnie Mouse thermos. "Fuck. I'm out. How long are we planning to wait for your contact to show up, Mack?"

"We've been here literally ten minutes, Jackson," my partner replied. "Maybe buy a bigger thermos that will carry the gallons of dark roast your addiction requires."

"Nope, I got this one at Disneyland two years ago when I took Leo. He picked it out. It's perfectly serviceable."

"Whatever. So, back to my piles," my partner said.

"Must we?"

"Yeah, because this is going somewhere. So, I asked Elena, after we cleared the table, if that was normal. Her family members being so into the personal lives and ailments of their new son-in-law, and she was like, 'oh, honey, you don't even know.' So I asked her why in God's sweet temperament she even told her mother that I had anal issues."

"Mack, honestly, this is past bordering on too fucking much information," I grunted, wiggled up, and tried to straighten my legs. "This car sucks."

"Don't talk that way about Penelope." He rubbed the steering wheel of the tiny ten-year-old Honda Civic as if it were his wife's breasts. "It's not her fault you're the same height as Shaq."

"Okay, no, I am not. Shaq is seven-one, and I'm only six-five." My back popped as I moved to try to get some feeling back into my lower extremities. "And you hate this car as much as I do. You admitted it just two weeks ago when you'd had that one extra beer after work. So why not trade it in for something that's not a fucking clown car so anyone over Hobbit-size might have some fucking leg room?"

He stared at me with those cornflower-blue eyes of his. "You are incredibly pissy today. I mean even more pissy than your usual pissy, which is, you know, damn pissy."

"We've been sitting here in the sun for over two hours waiting for this Twiggy dude to show up with some information. I'm out of coffee. And my fucking nicotine patch wore off."

"It's been ten minutes. Ten. Minutes."

"Whatever."

"Just an FYI, they don't wear off an hour after you— where the hell are you going?! Don't get out of the car. You'll stand out like a bull pecker, to quote my dear departed ma."

I flung the door open, unfolded my legs, and exited. I'd been Cormack Graham's partner for over two years, and in all that time, I'd never ceased to be amazed at the litany of inventive ways the Scots could describe things. His mother must have been a pistol.

"I need to get more coffee. I'm just going to the corner store right there," I explained before I closed the door on his protest. As if my getting out of the car was going to draw attention to us when a red-haired, pale-as-cottage-cheese goofball talking at full volume about his damn hemorrhoids hadn't already pulled the eyeballs of every damn soul on the street. We were on this busy street in Watts, sitting in a sunflower-yellow Honda Civic with Barbie bumper stickers that his lovely new bride had insisted be applied. And since Mack could deny Elena nothing… yeah. But it was me who would scare off Twiggy the rat.

I crossed the street at the light, stepped into the corner store, blinked at the change of bright to dark, then headed for the coffee pots sitting beside the slices of pizza in a case. The patrons and owner eyeballed me as I filled my Minnie Mouse thermos, then ambled to the cash register. I waited behind an elderly woman buying lottery tickets and began picking at the patch on my biceps as I held the thermos to my chest with my left arm.

"You want anything else?" the middle-aged man behind the register asked.

"Yeah, pack of Newports," I replied and pulled down my sleeve.

The guy stared up at me. "You know you ain't supposed to smoke while wearing a patch, right?"

"Your point?"

"Whatever." He tossed a pack of smokes at me, rang me up, and watched me leave. The sun was bright and hot as I made my way back to the totally inconspicuous banana-yellow Honda with the Barbie stickers. Mack waved at me as I neared, his freckled face tight with worry. I hurried to hide the cigarette pack in my pocket.

"I thought you were getting coffee." I raised my full thermos. "And what the hell is that cigarette pack-shaped bulge in your front pocket?"

"That's a sign of how much I fucking love you," I countered, pulling the passenger door open, then with a sigh of misery, cramming myself back into the passenger seat.

"Leo will be so disappointed."

"Him and all my exes."

"Call came from dispatch. There's been a mugging at the clinic over in Highland."

"And this concerns us how? Patrol will deal with it."

"Seems the victim has been having trouble with some of the local gangs in the neighborhood. Dispatch tagged us on it when the name Ivan Baladin was mentioned."

That made me look up from removing the patch. Ivan Baladin was a mid-level racketeering goon we'd been trying to nail for well over a year. He was just smart enough to ensure that those under him always took the fall for his crimes, but not quite smart enough to keep his pushed-in face completely off the radar—like his bosses and their bosses did.

"Okay, let's go talk to the doctor and see what he can tell us. Inform patrol that we'll be taking over the scene.

Lock it down until we get there. Any suspects apprehended?"

"Nope, but there was a witness who saw the offender up close and personal." He cranked the engine over, and Penelope rolled to life.

"Have them hold on to the witness, then do a neighborhood sweep. We'll want to question him. How's the victim? Can we get to him today?"

"On his way to the ER."

"Shit, okay. We'll get to him later."

I juggled my coffee while trying to open a pack of cigarettes, as we rolled through Watts at a goodly clip. We both had smaller portable radios on our person, but since I was fully occupied, Mack relayed that we were on our way to the scene, then added my directions. While Mack was the senior officer in our pairing—by two years—he tended to allow me to lead quite often. We were both pretty green in comparison to some of the homicide detectives in our precinct. Hell, we were babes compared to Mason and Berke, the elder goats in Organized Crimes. Our department was *extremely* short-staffed. Homicide used to have more teams but despite lots of murders happened in the City of Angels, now we had only ten cops to investigate all those cases landing in our district.

Of course, compared to Mason and Berke, anyone under the age of fifty was an infant, as they were both ready to retire within a year. Which would boost me and Mack to the top of the ladder in our department. Getting new blood into law enforcement was a hard sell nowadays. Lots of people couldn't hack it. Being a cop was not all glamour and witty repartee as it was on TV, which some cadets quickly learned, then dropped out. Lots of people just did *not* belong in a position of power that having a badge provided, and they were weeded out as well. Sadly, some slipped through the cracks.

So yeah, lots of reasons to cite as to why it was harder than a bull pecker, to quote Mother Graham, to get young people interested in being cops. It was easy to say we should defund the police, but when that resulted in budget cuts that decimated the ranks of those who were serving and protecting, the sheep stomach was boiled, also to quote Ma Graham. Mm, haggis. My gut growled. I should have grabbed a slice or two of the pizza to go with my coffee.

But hey, it was all good. Working a dozen cases at once was grand. Not as though me or my fellow officers needed a private life. Downtime was overrated. And sleep. Pfft.

Sleep was for sissies.

MACK PULLED UP BEHIND A SHINY DUCATI THAT MADE US both gape in wonderment.

"Is Tom Cruise filming a movie here or something?" Mack asked as the Honda sputtered into a stall, which was almost as good as a stop in my book. "Not a common make in these parts."

I glanced around the neighborhood but saw no signs of movie-making. One never knew when one lived in the land of movie stars. I'd seen my fair share of the bright and shiny people who glittered out here in Tinsel Town. Some were incredibly nice; some were flaming assholes. Like the rest of the population.

I exited the car with a moan, circled the expensive bike, then threw my partner a look as he worked at putting his tie back around his thick neck. I'd opted for cool today and had ditched a jacket and gone with khaki pants, a white shirt, and a tie I suspected had been doused with guacamole the last time I had worn it. It smelled like guac when the sun hit it.

Stretching to work out the kinks, I checked to make sure my weapon was secured in my holster, my badge was on my belt, and my thermos was in my hand.

"I hate ties," Mack grumbled as we entered the front of the clinic.

"Cap likes them," I replied, taking in the usual aura of upset following a crime. People white with fear, some crying, some pacing nervously, and some sitting in the waiting room with tension radiating off them. Two uniformed officers met us as we entered, both younger cops.

"Thanks for securing the scene. Are all of these people potential witnesses to the mugging?" I enquired and got two firm nods. Christ. There must be twenty people here. "Okay, cool. Any chance you've taken statements?"

A baby started to cry in the corner. The mother, a young Latina, bounced the bundle in the blue blanket, her dark eyes drifting shut despite her attempts to keep them open. I could relate. Not to the parenting thing. Gods, no. My sister was the Winwood who had kids. Just one, Leo, with my ex-brother-in-law, who... well, we'd not go into her reasoning for choosing Bryce back in the day. She'd been young. He'd had a guitar. You know how it goes. I'd disliked Bryce for a long time, for many reasons, but, as of late, we'd been working things out. Mostly for Leo's sake, as my nephew adored his dad.

But seeing as Court was newly married to a forest ranger named Tony, I suspected another addition to the family within a year or two. I, on the other hand, had trouble keeping the lone orchid Mack's wife had insisted I own alive, let alone a kid. Not that I didn't want kids someday, but I had zero time to date, let alone plan for offspring in some unforeseeable future.

We had a quick chat with the patrol officers about the people being detained. Many had seen little more than a man dashing through the waiting room. Those, we turned loose after taking a brief statement and reminding them to contact us if they remembered anything.

While Mack started taking statements from the staff—from the reception attendant named Lazlo Richter to an older woman, Heloise Grant, the bookkeeper, who just happened to be there to pick up paperwork—I found the room where the crime had taken place. An office belonging to the doctor in charge, one Joseph "Joe" Baxter, an ex-military medic who had returned from a few tours in the Middle East to open the Haven of Hope Clinic. A solid guy, do-gooder type, I assumed, which was commendable. God knows the poor areas of this city could use more help in every way, shape, or form. The room had been taped off by the patrol officers, so I ducked under the tape, careful to step over the spilled coffee and papers scattered about. Along the far wall were pictures of Joe the Medic with family, friends, and fellow Marines, as well as a few diplomas and a smudge of blood leading to a rather large puddle on the floor. According to the staff who had attended the victim, the head wound had been superficial. Head wounds were always messy. Mack and I would head to Holy Trinity Hospital after we were done here to see if the victim was able to speak to us.

Mack joined me to work on the preliminary documentation and evaluation of the scene. There had been way too many people in here to please me, but it was what it was. The responding officers had done a good job of taking care of the witnesses and bystanders who'd been secured and separated. I moved around the area another time, documenting as much information as possible while ensuring that scene integrity was in place, and all evidence was safe and uncontaminated.

Certain protocols had to be followed from the first arrival of the patrol officers to the scene debriefing team's final survey.

An hour later, we left Joe the Medic's office with not much to go on, other than that this was no botched robbery. This looked to be a warning of sorts, and according to the initial interviews, the name of a certain crime lord had been heard as the offender fled.

Then we split, Mack sitting down with the rest of the office staff to finish statements, while I sat down in an exam room with one Oliver "Cowboy" Cowan, defenseman for the LA Storm. I knew Oliver by sight and name, obviously. He would show up on occasion to help coach the youth teams that the Storm sponsored. My nephew was on such a team.

"Imagine seeing you here," I commented as the big D-man eyeballed me for the longest time, his sharp eyes moving over me, head to toe, as he tried to recall who I was, other than a gangly ass with a gun, a badge, and a Minnie Mouse thermos. "I'm Bryce's ex-brother-in-law. Jack Winwood, LAPD Organized Crimes Unit."

Nothing. Then the name hit him and some of the tension left his face. A handsome face that showed some life.

"Oh right, Michael Zhang's boyfriend. Sorry. I should have recalled his name sooner. It's been a day," he said, then stood. I waved him back to the chair he'd been sitting in and took a seat beside him. The room was decorated with duck and chicken decals for the little ones.

"So I heard." I settled down into my chair, my sight flickering to the tidy cabinets over a shiny sink. "Want to tell me about what happened?"

"I already told the other cops," he said, as I knew he would. "I'd really like to get to the ER to check on Joe."

"I know you spoke to the uniformed officers, but now I'd like you to tell me in your own words what happened." My sight flickered from Oliver to the room in a quick sweep. The cabinets were untouched, the shelves holding glass jars of swabs, cotton balls, and tongue depressors. So the offender had not rushed in, wired for dope, and started ransacking random rooms. The offender knew just where to go. Interesting.

"Organized Crimes?" That always got them once it sank in. His eyebrows knotted. "Why are you here? It was just a junkie looking for drugs, I assumed."

I gently unscrewed the cracked cup off the top of my

thermos. The AC kicked in. Ollie the Cowboy smelled damn good. Much nicer than stale guac and drying blood.

"We're not sure exactly what the offender was after. Can you start from the beginning, please?" I asked in my most polite cop tone. Considering I'd not had a chance to even light a cigarette yet, Ollie was indeed being blessed with all my charm. I placed my phone on the exam table, taking note that the paper covering was pristine. Yeah, random junkie my ass. "I'm going to record your statement, if that's okay with you?"

"Sure, yeah." He studied me closely with dark eyes. Christ, he was a good-looking beast of a man. Burly, yet toned, with short hair and neat scruff, both peppered with silver. I'd always enjoyed a good tumble with an older lover. We were of equal size and weight, although he might have a few pounds on me. Yeah, I could get down with going down on this man. "I just… can I call my kids' school to let them know that I'm going to be late picking them up?"

Well, shit. Shit on a rancid stick. Kids. So, he was taken. Probably had a hockey wife at home waiting for his return. I didn't know the Storm players or their personal lives, but being Leo's uncle meant I skated on the periphery of the team's activities.

"Sure. Go ahead." I leaned up, paused the recording, and sat back to nurse my now tepid coffee while Oliver took care of his kids. He spoke softly for such a big man. I wagered he would be a gentle lover, unless a man asked him to be rough, then—

For fuckin' fuck's sake, stop. The guy is straight. Man, we need to get laid.

Yep. We did need to get laid. Soon.

Oliver glanced at me, his gaze as weary as my body was.

"Sorry, that was… I didn't think I would be here this long. The girls are going to be worried about me not showing up."

"Feel free to call your wife to go get them."

Oh. Oh, Jackson, that was lame. So lame. So obvious.

"My wife died two years ago."

Fuck. I inhaled, then let it out slowly. "Sorry for your loss."

"Thank you, Detective. Can we get on with this?"

"Yes, of course." I dove into procedure to help bury the tremendous shame that overwhelmed me at that moment. Drooling over a widower with two daughters at a crime scene.

Yeah, I was heading to the nearest gay bar as soon as my shift was over.

Chapter Three

Oliver

I WAS SITTING ON A CHAIR IN AN EXAM ROOM SET UP FOR pediatric clients, surrounded by cheerful ducks, peeps, and bunnies scampering around the brightly painted walls, and there wasn't much else I could do. One of the cops had told me to stay—Mack, I think his name was—and the other one, Jackson, said I should arrange for the school to keep my girls. Then he'd left me to do what I needed to do.

I'd lied when I called. I told the school I was stuck at the arena— no way was I telling them anything about guns, guys with guns, blood, or the guy my girls called Uncle Joe now lying in the hospital. The school was fine with it and asked if there was someone else who could help me, and I immediately thought of Clare, our captain's wife. Their kids were at the same school, but much younger, and she'd already said there was a group of Storm wives who shared pickups. I was on my own, and I couldn't be there for my girls every moment, as much as I wanted to be, but I hadn't asked the group for help yet.

What if I didn't make it back to the school, and the girls were stuck there and…

I needed help.

I didn't know how long I had until the cop was back in here, so I quickly messaged the chat for the Storm players —my first message in there, actually—asking Cap for a number to call Clare. He was on the phone within a minute.

"You okay?" he asked me, without even a hello. Talk about taking captaincy a step too far. He'd gone into default fix-it mode in an instant.

"Your wife said if I ever needed help with the girls, I could ask. I can't pick them up from school on time. Would she pick up the girls for me and maybe take them out for pizza or something? I can pay."

"Fuck no," Cap huffed, and my stomach fell. Putting myself out there was hard enough without my teammates not helping me out. Then he carried on talking. "No way will she get them pizza, because don't get me started on e-numbers and carbs. She'll take them back to our place. I'll message you the address to pick them up. Is everything okay?"

Relief flooded me. "It's all good. I'm just running late."

"Sending you the address now. Call me if you need anything."

I didn't know what he meant by that, and I didn't really need anything except for the kids to be safe. The message arrived, along with confirmation that Clare was so happy to have more around the table.

I sent a message to my best friend—Jamie—asking

him how he was and that I wished he was here. He was in Australia right now lecturing at some kind of math symposium, and I wished he was here. I missed him like a limb. He'd paid his way through getting his doctorate by caring for my girls when I couldn't. He took on the nanny role when Melissa had been ill, and after she'd gone, he'd simply never left. I wished that I could have brought him from New York as easily as I'd brought my bike, just scooped him up into a box and packed him with everything else. Not only to care for the girls, though. He was my best friend, my sounding board, and the girls loved him. But he wasn't an inanimate object—he was someone who had his own life.

Jamie: What's wrong?

Oliver: Nothing

Jamie: What's wrong? And don't lie.

Oliver: Can't a bro miss a bro?

I added a stuck-out tongue emoji and imagined Jamie smiling. I didn't have a great emoji game, and he still hadn't gotten over the emoji shopping list I'd once sent him with eggplants on it. How was I to know? I was a hockey player, not an emoji-expert.

Jamie: Gotta go, sorry

My stomach fell. I was alone in this room and didn't even have Jamie to chat with. I hadn't gotten close to any of the Storm players yet, although Ash was a good guy, with his supply of candy in case I hypo'd on his watch, and his incessant need to call me old man. My head hurt, mind still reeling and the adrenaline slowly ebbing away, leaving cold shock in its wake. I checked my sugar levels, but my system was looking after me, and there was no way I was messing with that.

The cop walked back in. "Okay?" he asked, and I nodded as he sat down in the other chair, seriousness lingering around him like a second shadow. His voice was gruff, each word pointed, each question sharp, as if trying to carve the truth out of what I'd seen.

"So, take me back. You walked in on the scene?"

"Yes."

"And that's something you do? I mean, you have access?"

I tapped the card on the small table next to me. "I'm allowed. I volunteer here. I was taking Joe some coffee, and the files are families that might need some help." I tried to gather my scattered thoughts. "I was just cheering Joe up. He's been through a lot with the clinic here. But when I got here…" The image of Joe, pale and bleeding, flashed before my eyes.

Jackson caught the change in my expression. "Take your time," he said, his gruff expression softening for a moment before he composed himself back into the detective persona.

I cleared my throat, uncomfortable with how this vulnerability felt. "I knocked and came in. There was Joe, slumped over, and that… that guy pointing the gun. It all happened so fast." My hands clenched as if I could imagine Joe's blood still there.

"You didn't recognize the assailant?" Jackson asked, flipping through his notes. Our witness had short, kind of scruffy blond hair, along with a five o'clock shadow, and he was a long way past tired, his eyes bloodshot. He shifted in his chair again, and it creaked, because he was a big guy, broad and solid, and I was trying hard not to move on my chair to prevent the entire thing from collapsing. "Mr. Cowan?"

I snapped back to the questions. "Sorry, no, never saw him before."

"And can you describe him?"

"Skinny guy, lots of scars on his face, a neck tattoo that was just a blur, smiley face tattoo on his hand. Uhmm… I don't know if this matters, but he smelled as if he hadn't showered in days, and his dental hygiene was bad, and I mean *bad*."

"Everything matters, Mr. Cowan."

"Oliver. Please, call me Oliver."

He glanced up at me, as if he was going to argue, but then he nodded. "I'm Jackson."

"Okay."

"Do you remember what he was wearing?"

"Gang stuff maybe. T-shirt with no sleeves, grubby, blue I think, and dark pants that rode low. Belt, with a knife hanging off it, and the gun, of course." I shuddered as I recalled the asshole leaning over Joe, and the way Joe was fighting to stay conscious. "That's all I recall… wait… he wore Converse, old ones, he stepped in the…" In the blood. Nausea washed over me, and I swallowed hard. There was no way I was going to vomit in front of the grumpy, exhausted, but hot-as-fuck detective.

Hot?

Great, now my situational awareness was all messed up—no one thinks about how hot a cop is after an attempted murder. Right?

"*Promise me you won't stop looking.*" Melissa's voice filled my head—we'd always appreciated men together. Me being bi meant we had an entire world of guys to check out, and she made me promise to never stop looking. Grief shoved at my brain, and the single positive outcome was that it beat my nausea down a few notches. Grief was all-consuming and fucking hard to fight, but it was also incredibly powerful and knocked anything else I might feel on its ass.

"We have his shoe print," Jackson confirmed, and of course, they did. I bet they'd been over that office with a fine-toothed comb. "So, what conversation did you hear?"

"Well, I didn't hear what he and Joe were talking about, because Joe was already reeling from the blow to the head, uhm…" I blinked at him as I attempted to recall the exact words the assailant had used. "I asked him something. I don't know what. It could have just been a squeak, or I inhaled, or whatever. He told me to shut up, pointed the gun at Joe, and… and…" I could feel my heart pounding as the terror of the moment returning in a visceral rush.

"And what?" Jackson pressed, his gaze locking onto mine, unyielding and expectant.

I thought he was going to shoot Joe and then me. I hadn't seen my life flash before my eyes. None of that shit was true. I'd just seen the man's eyes as they narrowed.

"Brown eyes," I blurted. "He had dark brown eyes. I just remembered."

Jackson dutifully wrote that down.

I carried on. "Then, he left. Just ran out as if threatening people's lives was nothing to him." Anger surged at the memory, at the helplessness of it all.

Jackson nodded, scribbling something in his notebook. He glanced at me again, his gaze searching. "What did you do after he left?"

"I went straight to Joe. I caught him before he hit the floor." The feeling of Joe's weight against me was still too present, too real. "I called 911 right after. I didn't know what else to do."

"You did good," Jackson said, his voice not quite gruff now. It was an affirmation that sounded like something that rarely escaped his lips. "Then what?"

"I came out here, and that's when I found Heloise."

"That would be Heloise Grant, admin?"

"Yeah, the perp—do you even use that word?"

"Not really."

"Oh." I blinked at him. "Yeah, well, I heard banging, and she was locked in the janitor's closet, crying. I helped her out. She may have seen something I missed?"

"My partner is interviewing her."

"Okay."

"We'll take it from here. Just a few more questions and then, you can get your girls or go see Joe at the hospital."

"Thank you."

"What is the nature of your volunteering here?" he asked.

"Is that relevant?" I asked quickly.

My secrets were mine, and Jackson could well talk to his ex-brother-in-law, who'd talk to Michael Zhang, and then, he'd talk to his brother, Charles, and the entire team could know. I didn't want them to learn everything about me yet. I didn't trust anyone enough to explain. Yet.

We entered an epic stare-off, and then he shrugged.

"I'll just write volunteering," he said.

Jackson stood, his tall frame unfolding in the cramped space. "One last thing, Mr. Cowan. Did you notice anything else unusual? Anything out of place in the room? Any sign of drugs, or—"

"Joe has done nothing wrong. He wouldn't break the law if it meant saving his own life." I was damn fierce in his defense.

"I've seen the best people cross ethical lines for the strongest of reasons. Maybe Joe was dealing to get money for the clinic, maybe he'd made a deal with the local gangs to—"

"No. There are no deals, whatever you mean by that. The local guys come in with their families—they need this place as much as anyone else, sick parents, or kids who need help. This is a good place, and Joe is a good man." I stared at the cop, who was being an asshole. "Check your bias at the door, Officer," I snapped.

Jackson blinked at me, then his gaze softened for a second, and I could see a hint of empathy in his hardened gaze. I thought he might defend himself, but he just looked so damn tired, as if he'd seen so much that he couldn't see the good in things. I felt a twinge of sympathy, but kept it hidden.

"If you remember anything else, anything at all, call

me." He handed me a card with his number on it, and I knew I was scowling at him, but all he did was half-smile.

"I will," I said, taking the card gently and not snatching at it like my temper wanted me to.

As Jackson turned to leave, his steps echoing slightly in the hollow room, I realized one more thing.

"Detective Jackson," I called out before he left.

He paused at the door, peering back. "Yeah?"

"He said something to Joe before running out. 'Get the fucking codes!' I don't know what that means. I get it was a threat, but Joe was mostly out of it by then."

"Was he threatening you?"

I reared back. "Shit, no. He was shaking Joe."

Jackson gave a slight nod, pulled out his book, made a note, then, with a dip of his head, was gone. After he left, I was alone with the quiet hum of the fluorescent lights, the scent of ink and paper, and my temper began to ease.

Breathe in. Breathe out.

Heloise came over and sat next to me, her hands in knots, mascara blotchy under her eyes. We didn't talk for a moment, both lost in what had happened.

"I didn't see much," she murmured. "They kept asking, but…" Her voice dissolved into sobs. "He just shoved me."

Instinctively, I wrapped an arm around her small shoulders and pulled her into my side. I could do this—I could protect someone who needed protecting. That was my job.

"It'll be okay," I said. "They'll find the man."

"What if…" *What if Joe is hurt so badly he doesn't wake up? What if the bad guys come back?* I'd already put in a call to organize some security and had something in place from tomorrow. For the time being, we all needed to get home. Heloise's husband turned up and took her away, glancing back at me with a nod.

There were a few staff there when I left, but the clinic had been closed for the day. I sketched a wave at Lazlo, who was tapping away on a computer, a cop leaning over his shoulder. Normally, we'd exchange goodbyes, shoot the breeze if we had time, but he seemed as wrecked as I felt. There was another cop on the door, and we nodded. Then it was time for me to head home, grab the SUV, and get the kids.

I needed to see my girls.

I pulled into Charles and Clare's driveway a little after six, my hands still tight on the steering wheel. Parking the car, I let out a long breath and sat there for a moment, feeling as though I'd left a piece of myself back at the clinic. The day's events had sapped my energy, but I glanced up as the front door burst open and there they were—my gorgeous girls. Daisy came bounding down the steps, her blonde pigtails bouncing, those clear blue eyes, so much like her mother's, sparkling with the innocence of her seven years. Scarlett trailed behind and her darker hair, like mine, was loose in curls, but when she looked up and caught my eye, her mother's blue gaze shone from her face and my heart twinged with a familiar ache.

I pulled my shit together, stepped out of the car, and braced myself for the impact as two bundles of energy hit me with hugs. "Daddy!" they chimed, and the weariness melted away, replaced by the warmth of their embrace.

"How was your day, girls?" I asked, holding their hands as we walked back to the car.

"It was the best!" Daisy gushed. "Clare let us help make dinner, and I cut tomatoes!"

"And I found a spider!" Scarlett added, her face alight with the day's adventures.

I wasn't the biggest fan of spiders, or indeed of any creepy-crawlies, but Scarlett was going to be a professor of spider-ology one day, or so she'd informed me. I knew that if such a degree existed, Scarlett would be right there at the front of the line to sign up.

"I don't like spiders!" Daisy said and pouted.

"I didn't show you!" Scarlett defended.

"You were gonna!" Daisy protested.

Luckily, Clare came out behind them—her arrival cutting short the building spider debate—followed closely by Charles.

"Thanks for looking after them, Clare," I said gratefully.

She grinned at me. "It was fun. Any time."

We said our goodbyes, and soon enough, the girls and I were driving back to the rented house we were still settling into. There was the question of whether it would become our permanent home, with an option to buy after a year as part of my rental agreement. Still, with my contract only running for two years, and with the memories of New York still clinging to me, I couldn't think about putting down roots yet.

"Daddy, are we going to stay in this house forever?" Daisy's question from the back seat caught me off guard. How did she know I was thinking about that?

I glanced at her in the rearview mirror. "I like it."

"Me too," Daisy said.

"What do you think, Scarlett? Do you like it here?"

Scarlett was quieter, her expression thoughtful. "Can we go back to New York one day?" she asked, her voice small, but hopeful. "I miss Jamie and my friends."

My chest tightened at her question. New York was a lifetime away. "We'll see, sweetheart," I replied, keeping my voice even. "LA is our home for now, but we don't have to stay in this house."

Scarlett didn't look convinced, but she nodded, pressing her face to the window as the city lights began to twinkle on.

"Can we get a house with a pool like Clare and Charles have?" she asked after a pause.

I smiled then. If a pool would win her over, then sure, we'd get a pool.

"Give it a year, and we'll see."

I knew the decision about where we'd settle down would come, as all big decisions do, in its own time. Meanwhile, though, I had Scarlett smiling at the thought of a pool, and Daisy chatting away about their day, and it was enough to forget the horrific scene I'd witnessed.

Only when the girls were in bed, everything flooded back in the silence of my room.

"Think of something else," I muttered as I punched my pillow into submission. I lay down, closed my eyes, tried to empty my thoughts of everything that might keep me awake.

And I swear, my last thought was of a grumpy cop with tired green eyes.

Chapter Four

Jackson

THE DAY AFTER THE CLINIC INCIDENT, I WOKE UP WITH A mouth that tasted as if I'd licked the underside of the men's holding cell latrine. You know the dragon's breath is bad when you nearly gag yourself, inhaling the fumes wafting from your mouth as you snore/snort yourself awake.

I peeked to the left. Thank God the space was empty. The guy I'd hooked up with after shots of Jager had chased beers at the Fuchsia Flamingo had left. Sitting up slowly, my head thumping, I could smell the scent of sex clinging to the stuffy air in my little bedroom.

I pulled the sheets away to stare down at my dick. Still in the condom. How lovely. Oh well, at least we'd practiced safe sex. Go us. Grimacing at the thought of the mess the saggy rubber was going to leave on my dick, I eased out of bed, stumbled into the bathroom, and flipped on the light.

Big mistake.

The guy in the mirror coated with toothpaste speckles

looked like hell. No, even worse than hell. The deepest
slurry pits of hell. Yep, that was better. My hair was stiff,
my eyes baggy, and my prick was glued into a used
condom. I stared at my reflection. I appeared ten years
older than twenty-eight. Christ. I poked at the bags under
my eyes. Nothing like living the high life. Cheap booze,
cheaper men, and pulling double shifts in a job that few
respected. Courtney had always begged me to choose a
different career—as a big sister, she endlessly worried
about her baby brother. But no, I had to follow the family
path of law enforcement that my father and his father and
his father's father had chosen.

My bladder reminded me that I had yet to piss.
Wincing as tugging the dried condom yanked a few pubes
out, I chucked the messy thing into the trash. Then,
because my cleaning lady would be coming today, I dug it
out, wrapped it in toilet paper, and stuffed that into an
empty toilet paper tube. Yep. Hashtag Glamorous Life.
Pfft.

I brushed my teeth for ten minutes, showered for five,
and somehow found my way to my kitchen for coffee. My
apartment was one of about twenty in a renovated building
supply warehouse, in a low rent area about two blocks
from the Northeast Police Station I called home. I had
spent more time there than I had here over the past two
years. To be honest, the new building that the taxpayers
bitched about steadily was homier than this one-bedroom
shithole of a bachelor pad.

My sister would explode if she saw how I lived. The
place was the same as it had been the day I'd moved in.
Nothing on the walls, no curtains, just the battered blinds,

and two pairs of sheets that Luisa changed monthly if I paid her more to do so. Smart woman. I'd not want to touch my sheets either, given some of the random men I'd fucked on them. Yanking open the fridge, I found milk, sniffed it, shrugged, and went to pour it over some cereal —when I realized that I didn't have any cereal. Right. That required shopping. Well, fuck. I'd run through a fast-food drive-in on the way and grab something greasy with zero nutritional value.

I lit a cigarette. That had to have some kind of nutrient, right?

Padding about with questionable milk and a smoke, I took a swig from the container, found my phone resting on the wireless charging dock, and picked it up. I scanned social media quickly and spent a few minutes reading about a wild party in the Hills that got busted for underage entertainment. I ground out my cigarette butt in an ashtray on the window ledge. This building had a no-smoking policy. Which always made me sarcastic-laugh. A smoke was a no-no, but selling drugs in the lobby was fine. The fact that I was a cop meant little. The little shits would scatter like cockroaches when the lights came on when I entered the lobby to check my mail. There were too many to chase. If you arrested one, the next day, some poor kid trying to survive would be taking the previous dealer's place. Hand to God, there were days we all felt like throwing in the towel. But then, we'd shake off the helpless feeling and go do our jobs.

I scoped out the names of the affluent individuals mentioned in the headlines. Ah, the rich and famous. Tossing the rest of the milk down, I got dressed, pulling on a pair of brown slacks, a tan shirt, and a tie with a bumblebee on it that Leo had gifted me last Christmas. I ran my fingers through my hair, pulled on some socks and my lone pair of brown dress shoes, and geared up. Gun, badge, phone, sunglasses, lingering shame of vapid sex, and a hangover. Perfect. I was ready to greet the public. Poor public.

I PULLED UP TO THE STATION WITH A JUMBO CUP OF DARK roast in my Minnie thermos and a bag filled with egg sandwiches with those delightful hash brown patties. Mack was waiting in the parking lot, talking on his phone, his red hair like a freaking scarlet beacon with the bright California sun shining on it. He glanced up when he saw my classic Riviera ease into a space far too narrow and short for my beauty of a car.

"No, hey, just run over my feet," he called as I exited the gold Buick. "Are those doughnuts?" He waved his cell at the bag in my hand.

"Why the need to play into stereotypes?" I shook the bag. "It's a totally unhealthy breakfast."

"Damn, I was hoping it was doughnuts. Elena is on this health food kick and has banned all sugary sweets from the house."

"And that is why I do not have a wife," I replied, entering the precinct with nods to the cops filing in and out, some plainclothes, some uniformed, all tired.

"I thought it was because you were gay," he fired back,

typing and walking as we hit the elevator to ride to the second floor.

Two older cops—CHiPs—eyeballed me as we rode up, the gay comment taking the ride with us. I assumed the motorcycle patrolmen were here to partner on a case. The LAPD and California Highway Patrol did work together sometimes: DUI checkpoints, for example.

"That too," I said as we exited on the correct floor of the mirrored building. The two staties said nothing, but their glowers could be felt until the doors on the elevator closed. That was not a unique reaction among older cops finding out there was a queer in the ranks. They'd get over it, like they did when Blacks, Latinos, and women were mainstreamed into the ranks of those in blue. Not that I wore blue, but… whatever.

Organized Crime had a small section of desks facing south. Homicide had more room with more desks. That was fine. No matter where you went, police stations all had that *Hill Street Blues* vibe. Or maybe that was just in my head.

I nodded to a few cops at the water fountain as Mack and I made our way to our desks. I'd just placed my bag of deliciousness on my desk when I got a shout from the captain of detectives.

I glanced at Mason, sitting at his desk with a newspaper spread out over the top. "Touch that and die, old man," I said and got a middle finger from the Detective III sitting in the bright sun like a turtle on a sunning log. Mack and I were both Detective I rank. *Wee babes*, as Mack liked to say when he was feeling his Scots.

Mack sat at his desk, across from mine, and returned to his phone as I ambled into the captain's office, stopping halfway through the door with my thermos in hand. Captain Franks looked up from his desktop, waved me in, then sat back as I closed the door and parked my ass. His space was tidy as a fucking nunnery. Nothing out of place, which was exactly how Franks was as well. He always dresses neatly in a pressed suit, with a shaved head and a beard tightly trimmed to his square jaw. His dark eyes were sharp like a dagger.

"You look like something my wife scooped out of the cat's litter box," Cap said as soon as the door was closed.

"I've only had half a thermos of coffee and two smokes. Come see me when I'm fully rejuvenated around noon. I'll be a brand-new man."

"Thought you were quitting," he said, sitting back in his squeaky chair, then folding his hands over his expanding belly. His days of chasing criminals through the wild streets of Los Angeles were firmly behind him. As was evidenced by how large his behind was getting, too.

"So did I. Did you want something in particular or did you call me in here to admire my good looks? I will say that Isobel will not like you making passes at me."

"My wife makes more passes at you than I ever could."

I chuckled. That was true. Isobel Franks was a scandalous woman with a heart of pure gold. She had taken me under her wing the first time I'd met her, and she found out I was queer. She'd smashed my face into her substantial bosom at the captain's yearly Fourth of July cookout for the men under him and told the rest of the idiots I worked with that if they wanted to come at me, they would have to go through her.

Not that I needed her protection. I was used to taking care of myself, but that kind of motherly attention was nice. I didn't get it often.

"I got a call from a hockey player on the Storm." He shuffled some papers, found his reading glasses, then fastened them to his large ears. "Oliver Cowan. Dispatch sent the call to me, as you weren't in yet and weren't replying to calls."

Oh right, yeah, I'd turned my phone off when I had planned to get shitfaced then laid, in that order, last night. I'd not checked my text log when I had rolled out. Seemed more prudent to see what kind of new chicken videos were all the rage on TikTok after checking on the movie stars being arrested.

"My battery was dead. Did he say what he wanted?" I sat a little straighter. Oliver had been on my mind all day, and most of the night, until I'd gotten drunk enough to force him from my thoughts.

"Not precisely, only that he wanted to speak with you at your earliest convenience. Is he related to that clinic robbery yesterday? I don't have your paperwork." The flat look he shot me over the top of his glasses spoke fucking volumes. Guess I knew what I was doing this morning. Fucking reports. Maybe I could get Mack to do mine if I gave him a hash brown...

"Sorry, I got into something last night," I mumbled, then quickly filled my supervisor in on what I had so far about the clinic robbery/mugging. "Seems the offender was there to deliver a message to the clinic owner. Sounds like typical strong-arm stuff that Baladin is known to employ." I read over my notes on my phone. "The assailant exited the clinic at a fast pace, shouting to the patients in the waiting room about Baladin coming down hard on assholes." I glanced up at Cap, who was processing. "Why he was tossing his boss's name around, I don't know. I' bet he was tweaking and running his mouth to sound even tougher. Mack and I are going to the hospital today to talk to this Joe Baxter as soon as we get cleared by the doctors. They wouldn't let us in to see him after the incident, so we'll swing over there today."

"*After* you hand in your reports."

"Sure, yeah, after that. I'll call Cowan as soon as I return to my desk."

"Okay, make sure you do. And do not leave this building without turning in your paperwork tome. I mean it, Winwood."

"Yep, on it now. Here I go."

I rose, tapped my brow with my thermos, and returned to my desk. Mack was typing away when I sat down. My bag seemed untouched. I opened it, dug in, and pulled out a hash brown. Mack's gaze rose from his laptop to the tater goodness in my hand. His pupils widened in pure lust.

"Damn it, they gave me an extra hash brown." They didn't. I had ordered four to go with my three egg and muffin sandwiches, but desperate times called for desperate measures. "I'll toss this your way, and never tell your wife that you ate takeout if you do my field reports from yesterday."

He called me a dozen dirty names, insulted my clan even though I was not Scottish, and then took the hash brown from between my fingers like an eagle swooping on a beached salmon. Fare thee well deep-fried potato vivaciousness.

"I hate you," Mack said around a mouthful of spud. His lips were slick with grease. He looked incredibly happy.

"You love me, and you know it," I countered as I dialed the number Oliver had given me with his contact information yesterday. He picked up on the first ring. "Hello, Mr. Cowan; it's Detective Winwood returning your call."

"Thank you for calling back. Is there a way to talk to you privately? I'm at the barn right now."

I heard the din of many male voices on the other end.

"Sure, I'd be happy to come to your farm."

"No, not a farm. Barn. Sorry. Hockey-speak for a rink."

"Ah, right? I knew that."

"Morning skate will be over in about an hour. Can we meet for coffee somewhere?"

"Is this about the clinic case? Did you remember something important?"

"I think…well, I think it might tie in, but I'm not sure."

To be honest, I'd have driven to any farm the man might have been at. Fucking Robby Rando last night was supposed to cure the itch I felt when this man's voice entered my ear. Since I was half hard already, the sex last night must have been dismal. I didn't recall any of it, but obviously, it hadn't worked. I did a quick search of food places near the arena.

"That will work fine. Why don't we meet at noon at that steakhouse a block down from the arena?"

There was a moment's hesitation before he replied. "Yeah, sure, that'll work. Noon then. I'll reserve a table outside."

"Okay. See you then." I was tempted to say his name at the end, but he hung up before I could hit him with all my fierce game. Not that I should be using his first name in any kind of familiar way, obviously. That would be unprofessional. I chewed on a chilly egg and muffin sandwich that was dripping cheese onto the bumblebee on my tie, and my mind enjoyed the way his name sounded.

I made a mental note to change my tie before I went to meet him.

Chapter Five

Oliver

TODAY WAS A SHORT PRACTICE, BUT THE DAY AFTER tomorrow we would fly to an away game, and that was still a bone of contention with Scarlett and Daisy. They'd wanted to come, but it was the middle of a school week.

At least, Jamie coming here would make them happy, my best friend and their former nanny was visiting on my dime to take care of the girls for me, and I missed him so much that I was as excited as the girls to see him. I wished the excitement wasn't dampened by thoughts of what had happened yesterday.

And now, I was meeting the cop—Jackson, he of the pretty eyes and the surly attitude—because I'd seen something else.

I think.

Only, what I'd seen was a stupid detail, and really, had I just imagined it, or even seen anything at all? Maybe I should have talked to Joe first, but he was still unconscious —swelling of the brain, according to Lazlo, who'd answered my message at four a.m. He was close with Joe's partner, and at least he had access to information—the hospital were waiting for the swelling to ease, but they were hopeful everything was okay.

Seemed like Lazlo hadn't been able to sleep either.

What if it had been worse? What if that guy had shot Joe? What if I'd walked in on a murder? Would he have killed me as well? What would've happened to my girls if I'd gotten hurt? My will stated that Jamie would have guardianship. I knew he loved the girls, and I knew he'd agreed, but did I want to leave them the same as their mom? What if—

"Heads up!" someone shouted, and I got a face full of wet towel, which was enough to snap me out of my worries.

"The fuck?" I yanked the towel off my face, ready to wreak vengeance on whoever had done this, only to come face to face with Cap himself, who was grinning ear to ear.

"Still got the aim," he announced to the room, but no one said anything because there was no one there.

It was me and him. Somehow, the rest of the team had finished getting dressed and left, and I was still sitting in my cubby, lost in thought.

"Are you going home?" Charles asked, sitting in the next cubby and knocking my leg with his.

"Yeah, sorry. I was just thinking…" I shrugged.

"If you're worried about being here, then I've gotta say, I really admire the way you play. You've got this style; it's like classic hockey, you know? Just gritty and real."

A small smile found its way onto my lips. I'd always taken pride in my style of play: nothing fancy, simply good, honest hockey. "I just play the game the only way I know how," I replied.

"And it's good, so yeah, you don't need to worry about the hockey, if that's what's got you spaced out."

Ah, this was why it was Cap sitting next to me—he'd thought I needed a pep talk. Maybe I did—maybe I needed to hear that I was doing okay, but it wasn't that which had made me sit so quietly like an idiot.

"Sorry, just a lot on my mind. I fit here on the team."

"You do." He frowned. "So, if it's not hockey stuff, what is it? Is it the girls? Clare asked me to ask you if you needed help with them over the next few days. They could always stay at our house if you're struggling to find a nanny?"

My heart filled with happy then. I'd worried about how I would fit in with the team, but from the captain down, everyone had been so welcoming and supportive.

"Actually, their old nanny is on his way back from a work placement in Australia, and he's stopping and staying with them."

"Wow, that's a long way to go to cover childcare."

"Jamie is more than just a nanny," I said without thinking that maybe I needed to qualify that.

"'More than just a nanny', eh?"

I glanced at Charles, and he was grinning.

"No, not like that. He's my best friend, and the girls love him."

"Okay, so you have childcare this time, but you know, if there's some way we can help, or you have anything else you want to talk about, you know where I am, right?" Charles tapped the phone he was holding.

"Sure, Cap."

He stood and stretched, wincing as he raised his left arm. "Jeez, do you ever think you're getting too old for this game?" he asked.

I smirked. "Never."

By the time I was slipping on shoes and doing one last check on my hair, it was nearly time to meet the cop. And that was when I started second guessing his suggestion to meet at a steakhouse, of all things. I pulled up maps, found the place he'd suggested, tucked away on the side road, and I was there with ten minutes to spare, glancing at the open seating area and telling the server that there was a booking.

The table was right on the edge of the seating area, and I sat facing the restaurant, sipping water, checking the menu, and wondering if this was a brunch thing, a steak thing, or maybe a 're-not-eating-anything' coffee.

He arrived ten minutes later, a yellow Honda spitting him out onto the sidewalk. The car parked, and he leaned in, giving attitude to whoever was driving, who then drove off. Jackson weaved through tables to get to me, giving a wave to the server, who smiled at him. Did she know him? Was he a regular here? I'd seen him at practices before, so I guessed he knew the area, but the thought that we were meeting at a regular spot for him made me feel uneasy.

Like this wasn't me telling him what I thought I'd seen.

"Mr. Cowan," he said as he took the seat facing the street, shuffling his chair so he was more on the corner and could see the restaurant as well. He seemed just as tired as he'd been yesterday, if not worse, and his day-old stubble had become two-day stubble, and he'd bitten his lower lip somehow, then worried at it, so it looked sore. I assumed that, between yesterday and now, he'd showered, given his hair lay in fluffy layers and he smelled of cedar and heat.

I'm smelling what now?

"Call me Oliver, or Oli, or hell, Cowboy, if you want, but please, drop the Mr. Cowan," I deadpanned.

The server came over and, without even checking the menu, Jackson spoke up. "The Blue Burger, no onions. Leave the salad, please, but extra fries, and water," he said with a smile that the server returned. The server was smiling way too hard, and I felt a pinch of…

Of what? Jealousy? Fuck's sake, Oliver.

At least Jackson was ordering food, and my rumbling belly told me I needed food too.

"Chicken salad, hold the dressing, side plain pasta, and I'll stick with the water, as well," I ordered.

She left with another smile and then, it was only me and Jackson.

"Do you always meet witnesses in restaurants?" I asked and leaned on my elbows, daring him to lie to me.

"Yes," he muttered gruffly, then cleared his throat. "No, not really. But I needed to eat, and this is close to where you were. I have an hour."

"Well, it's probably nothing, and this meeting might be a waste…"

"Why don't you let me be the judge of that?" The server returned with the water and sashayed away, but I noticed he didn't watch her leave.

"I think the guy with the gun took a photo from the

51

board behind Joe." That came out in a rush, and I sat back. Now, he was going to laugh me out of the restaurant.

"Go on," he encouraged, settling into the chair and leaning back as if he had all the time in the world.

The detail from the clinic that had nudged its way forward in my mind in the small hours of this morning after I'd gotten off the phone with Lazlo—a detail that had seemed insignificant at the time—had suddenly become all I could think about.

Was the photo important? Who the fuck knew, but the man with the gun… before he shouted about codes in that do-it-or-die threat, had hesitated and glanced at something in his hand. It could have been simply because someone had interrupted what he'd been doing, or it could have been something else. It was a photo of Joe with a group of staff from the clinic all smiling on some happier day, one that normally was on the bulletin board behind Joe's desk, and he was holding it.

I realized then—there was something else in the gunman's eyes. A flicker of something that went beyond the desperation of the moment, or the evil threat.

"It was a photo that Joe kept up on his board." I moved my fingers to approximate the size and glanced up to see him staring at my hands. "A picture of Joe and some staff on a hike, the first one they did to raise money way back. At least, that is what he said it was a picture of. I mean, I didn't recognize half the people in the photo." I shrugged. "But did the guy with the gun know Joe? Or someone in the photo?"

Jackson tugged out his phone, and for a moment, I thought I'd lost him. He scrolled, then placed the phone on the table, turning it to face me. The photo was a crime scene photo, not official, a little blurry, as if he'd taken it on his phone—was he allowed that on his phone? Hell, was I even supposed to see these?

I was at the damn scene, idiot; I've already seen it.

"That's the board, and the photo was where?" he asked and leaned over the phone, so our heads were almost touching. That scent of his, the stubble, the sore lip, his green eyes so focused, and I swallowed hard. *Head in the game, Cowboy.*

I peered closer, then gestured to a space on the side. "If I remember right, that was where it was. Do you think the armed guy taking it is significant?"

Jackson sat back in his chair. "Could be. It's a thread, a thin one perhaps, but something that might be worth pulling."

Food arrived then, and he dived into his burger as if he hadn't eaten all day. Which maybe he hadn't. Was anyone looking after him? He had sauce on his tie; he was exhausted. Maybe he needed someone to get him to stop with the self-destruction and get a life.

Says the man who fights grief and spends all his free time working out so he can play a game he's falling out of love with.

"Oodurger," he mumbled around a mouth of food, and I translated it as "good burger".

"I've never eaten here before." I thought I'd go with some conversation, but he never got to answer, or expand on what a cool place it was, or why he knew the menu so well. A car parked with a press of the horn, at the same time as Jackson's phone vibrated and moved on the slippery tablecloth.

"Let's go!" someone called from the car—the same cop from yesterday, the younger one, Mack.

After muttering "shit," Jackson quickly gathered what was left of his burger, grabbed a handful of fries, then stared at the table.

"I've got this," I said.

"I'll call you," he said, then left with a "sorry" and a "later." The car vanished, and the entire restaurant went from staring at him to chatting again.

I finished my lunch, paid the check, and headed home. I'd done my bit—told the cop what I thought. Not much else I could do now.

I hoped he got to finish his burger.

Chapter Six

Jackson

"Not to sound like my wife…" I threw a look at my partner as we crawled our way towards the hospital, my mouth so full of fries I probably appeared like an unkempt Rescue Ranger. "But if you chewed your food, you'd get more satisfaction from it. Also, and this is proven…" He stopped at a red light next to a beater Ford packed full of kids listening to Bad Bunny. The thumping beat made my fillings throb, which did not go well with the lingering headache I was enjoying. "Chewing one hundred times helps you feel more full."

The teens flipped me off. I returned the gesture. Today was not the day, kids. They sped off as my partner droned on about exercising your choppers.

"Ever since you got married, I don't recognize you," I said around the last bite of my burger. Mack glanced my way in shock. "No, hear me out." I burped into my hand. "Oof, onions. Okay, so before you tied the knot, we'd talk about good stuff. Like sex."

"I am not discussing my sex life with you. Elena wouldn't like it."

I pointed a finger coated with mustard at him. "See, that's what I mean. Now we talk about your piles, or your mother-in-law, or how many times a man should chew his burger. Is that what married life is all about? Hemorrhoids and mastication? Because if it is, I am so glad I've never fallen in love."

I stuck my finger into my mouth to clean off the mustard. Mack made a quick left as he stewed on my words.

"Do you want to talk about sex?" he finally asked as we pulled into the packed parking lot of Holy Trinity Hospital.

"No, not really. You'll have to go to the upper lot." I went to wipe my wet finger on my tie, then saw that I had forgotten to dig a cleanish tie out of my desk drawer before leaving to meet with Oliver. "Shit, I wore this tie to lunch. Why didn't you remind me to change it?"

"What am I? Your wife? Shit, I hate trying to find a place to park here."

"How dare all these people get sick?" I quipped. Mack shot me a look. "Try the upper lot."

"This *is* the upper lot."

"Try the *upper* upper lot."

"Maybe I should just slap the flasher on top of the roof."

"Nah, don't do that. Last time someone used their red and blues to get through the line entering a Lakers game, Cap gave them desk duty for a year."

"Oh yeah, Kendall. I remember him. He transferred out

to La Jolla. Nice house. The wife and kids love it out there."

My sight flew from my dirty tie to my partner. "Don't you even *think* about going suburban on me, Mack. Oh there, on the right of that Pontiac."

"Got it." He whipped into the slot, parked, and exited. I took off my tie, then rummaged in Mack's glove box for another. Elena kept about ten in there, all rolled up neatly as those puff pastry pinwheels she packed for his lunch. Maybe having a significant other wasn't all bad. Clean ties and baked goods were okay.

"Nice tie," Mack commented as we entered the front doors of the hospital. We got as far as the first nurses' station before being told that Mr. Baxter was unable to receive visitors. We flashed our badges. The overworked woman behind the desk stared at me flatly. Right.

"Do we know when Mr. Baxter will be awake to speak with the police?" I asked, eyeballing a guy bouncing a wailing baby on his hip. I'd arrested that guy once. Gang-related issues, stabbing a rival gang member outside a corner store in East LA, and now, here he was with a sick kid. His gaze met mine. He spun on his heel and bounced that crying baby all the way down the corridor and out of sight.

"As soon as the doctors say so," she informed us, then waved at the people in line behind us. Mack and I left, stepping out into the sunny day. The palms swayed. The clouds rolled past overhead. The sound of an ambulance careening into the ER entrance on the other side of the hospital floated by.

"Okay, well, next step. The lunch I had with Oliver

was fruitful," I said as we made the long-ass hike to that stupid yellow Honda.

"Oh, it's 'Oliver' now?"

I ignored the comment but took note of the familiarity and corrected mentally. "Mr. Cowan recalled seeing the offender with a picture from a bulletin board in his hand as he made his escape." We paused at a crosswalk to let an elderly man push his wife across the road. The wheelchair got stuck in a pothole, so Mack and I lifted the old gal free, then gently set her on the sidewalk. Both of them gushed about what fine men the LAPD had working for them. Mack and I blushed, then returned to our hike. "Take a look."

I showed him the photo I'd taken during the initial sweep we'd made of the scene.

"Huh, that's odd. I wonder if he was trying to hide something that he or someone he is close to was involved in. What did Cowan say the image was of?"

"Some sort of fundraising hike they did for the clinic a few years back. We might be able to run some facial recognition if we could find another copy of the photo."

"Or we could go to the clinic and talk to Lazlo Richter. He's the reception guy with blue hair. Seemed very willing to talk to us yesterday."

"Why don't we do both?"

"You could reach out to Timothy."

I groaned. Timothy was an evidence technician with the force. Nice guy, I guess, but desperate to get into my bed. Even a horn dog like me had some lines in the sand. Fucking a guy you worked with frequently was never a good thing. I'd not call him back for a second go, and he would get pissy, fingerprints would get lost, which would sabotage a potential case, and then I would have to punch Timothy-the-tech in the nose. I'd get fired. Timothy would sue. And I'd end up living in a rundown trailer on the beach, just like Jim Rockford.

"Yeah, no. Shit." That *would* speed things up. I glanced at Mack with big puppy eyes.

"Nope. I'm not doing it. I did all the paperwork this morning."

"I gave you a hash brown."

He stood firm. I cussed him and his kilted forefathers, then sent a text to Timothy asking if he would do me a huge favor. The reply was an enthusiastic yes if I would meet him for a margarita some night. I agreed. Some night could be tomorrow or in ten years. If nothing else, I was a master at avoiding romantic entanglements.

"He's on it."

"He'd like to be on you."

"Just drive us to the clinic before I tell Elena you snuck a hash brown."

Mack murmured under his breath all the way to the Haven of Hope clinic. We ambled in. The place was up and back in business, although the aura was subdued. Sitting behind the glass panel at the reception desk was a lean guy with vibrant blue hair, pale blue eyes, and a spiky earring in his left lobe. He was dressed corporate casual. His eyes flared when he spied us coming towards him.

"Mr. Richter, do you remember us?" I asked and got a nod. "Good. If you have a minute, my partner and I would like to ask you some questions."

"Umm sure?" He called out to a harried-looking older

woman in a pink sweater. She took his seat while staring at us openly. "Through that door." Lazlo pointed at a door in the waiting room. We nodded, pushed through, and met him on the other side. "We have a room open down here."

As we tagged along behind the office worker, the hushed sounds of people talking behind closed doors met us. A baby cried down the hallway. The place smelled of cleanser. Strong cleanser. The door to Joe's office was still taped off. Lazlo gave the yellow tape a glance, then rushed past it, as if to outrun the memory of the day before.

"In here." We stepped into your standard exam room. No duckies on the wall in this one, just posters asking where your pain tolerance was. I stared at the sad face for number six and could relate. I really needed another couple of Tylenol. Lazlo stood while we sat, his thin arms folded protectively over his chest. "Is Joe dying?"

"Not that we're aware of. We're here to see if you can shed some light on the photo in the background here?" I pulled out my battered Android, flipped through a hundred or so shots, then held up the image of the bulletin board that Lazlo had found. It was a little blurry given the photo had been taken of Joe sitting at his desk from a year ago, but it was the best we had. Mack sat beside me, recording the questioning. "Do you remember that photograph?"

Lazlo bent over to stare at the screen. "Oh sure, that's the first Haven of Hope Clinic Hike. That was before I started working here, but we do it every year. A bunch of us will drive out to Mount Baldy and do the trails."

"Sounds nice. Can you tell us who the people in this image are?" I asked once more.

"Are they in trouble?" Lazlo enquired, the eagerness to help now feeling tempered.

"Not at all. We'd just like to touch base with everyone who worked here or knew the victim to ensure we've not missed a potential clue."

He seemed okay with the standard cop sidestep. I wasn't about to divulge any information to someone who might let something slip. We liked being a step ahead of the criminals, if at all possible. Not that the people in the snapshot were criminals, but one learned really quick not to ignore any possibility. Sometimes the most innocent-looking people were the most dangerous.

"Most are employees. A few have moved on," he explained, his shoulders up around his ears. He was getting tense.

"Any family members?" Mack asked as I worked up my best hangover smile.

"Not in that picture," Lazlo replied stiffly. "I know that Joe takes it down sometimes and has it on his desk, but maybe he's just reliving the memory or… look, if someone is in trouble…"

"No one is in trouble." I stood slowly. "We're just looking into all possibilities. Could you possibly get us a list of the people in this photo? Names, addresses, that sort of thing. It would save us a lot of time compared to doing it back at the precinct."

"Okay sure." He seemed displeased to do as requested, but ten minutes later, we had a list of the people who were in that missing photo. "Heloise might know more about who's in the photo; she's been here longer than me."

"On it," Mack said and wandered away to find the poor woman from the closet.

I met Mack back outside, the sun making me squint, so I put my sunglasses back on and waited to see if he had anything to add.

"Nothing more to add to what Lazlo told us," he said. "She gave us the same names he did, in between crying."

I wanted to feel sympathy, but we really needed names.

"So, out of the ten people in the old photo, only one is working today? A nurse, Belinda Waters."

"Yep, I asked her to come find us after finishing with her patient."

She arrived as if we'd conjured her, a small woman who looked close to retirement. She didn't have much to add. She remembered the photo, knew it was something Joe kept on his board, didn't recall anything special happening the day it was taken, and that was it.

We'd talked with her for about five minutes before she was called off to assist a stand-in physician from the medical center two blocks over.

"Shall we spend the rest of the afternoon visiting these hikers?"

"Elena said to be home by six."

I assured him we would be done by then.

We weren't. He got bitched at, but got fed. I got to go home and spend the night with a dead orchid and a microwave meal.

Who was the winner in that scenario?

Chapter Seven

Oliver

THE NEXT MORNING, I MADE BREAKFAST MECHANICALLY, my thoughts not on the scrambled eggs or the toast, but somehow, after yet another restless night, I was replaying the attack, and the blood, and the hateful threats to Joe, plus a whole load of other things that left me feeling antsy. In among all that were green eyes and a tired smile and stubble, and hell, only Daisy and Scarlett chatting about their plans for the weekend with Jamie stopped my thoughts from spiraling, their voices a comforting buzz in the background.

"Daddy, you're burning the eggs!" Daisy's voice cut through my thoughts.

I snapped back to the present and stared at the pan, where the once yellow eggs had taken on a decidedly brown tinge.

"Ah, shoot," I muttered, taking the pan off the heat and scraping the contents into the garbage. "Sorry, Daisy. Guess I got a bit distracted."

Daisy climbed onto a stool at the kitchen counter, her feet swinging.

"It's okay. Can I have cereal instead?" she asked, her bright smile enough to brush away all the dark parts.

I tried to avoid too much sugary cereal for them, but hell, I'd burned the damn eggs, so cereal was a good option.

"Of course, munchkin," I replied, ruffling her blonde hair as I reached for the cereal box with its colorful cartoon character on the front.

I poured her a bowl, guided her as she added milk, the tip of her tongue poking out in concentration, and watched her dive in with enthusiasm.

"Did you burn the eggs, Dad?" Scarlett asked from the door, dramatically sniffing the air like a detective on the trail of a culinary crime.

I turned from the blackened skillet, feigning shock. "Burned? No, these are just… well, extra crispy. A new recipe I'm trying out," I said with a grin, hoping she'd buy into my playful excuse and give me one of her smiles, the same as Daisy had.

She eyed me, then smirked. "Extra crispy, huh? Is that what we're calling it now?"

Oh, the sass was strong in this one, and I loved it.

"Yeah, it's a delicacy in some places, you know? I'm just bringing you the finest dining experience. Only the best for my girls." I opened the window to let out some of the smoke, and Scarlett laughed, her earlier pretend investigation dissolving into giggles.

"Next time, can we try the not burned experience?" Scarlett asked.

I nodded in mock solemnity. "Absolutely, chef's promise. Now, how about some expertly poured cereal instead?"

She nodded, still chuckling. "I think that's a safer bet, Dad."

As I watched her take her seat at the table, the burnt breakfast incident already turning into a shared joke, I leaned against the counter with my coffee, grateful for this moment of normalcy, for Daisy's forgiveness over something as simple as breakfast.

All too soon, it was time to go to the airport to pick up Jamie. The girls were hyper, so excited to see Uncle Jamie, and their enthusiasm was infectious. I leaned against the barrier at Arrivals, Daisy and Scarlett bouncing on the balls of their feet beside me, their excitement practically electric in the air. Their eyes were wide, scanning the sliding doors every time they parted.

"There he is!" Scarlett squealed, her voice rising over the hum of the crowded airport as Jamie finally emerged. His dark hair was a little longer than the last photo he'd sent us, and he was wearing his '*I'm English Where's The Tea*' T-shirt. He was also apologizing—a lot, even by his British standards—as he attempted to guide a cart with at least six precariously balanced suitcases and to not kill any of his fellow passengers.

The girls ran toward him before I could say a word, wrapping Jamie in an embrace that nearly bowled him over. His laugh, warm and loud, filled the surrounding space, and I couldn't help but smile.

"Uncle Jamie, did you bring us anything?" Daisy's

voice was muffled against Jamie's chest, as she refused to let go.

"Did you see any kangaroos?" Scarlett's question followed immediately.

Jamie set his bags down and knelt to their level, opening his arms to enclose both girls in a giant hug. "I might have a thing or two in my suitcases." He winked at Daisy, then turned to Scarlett. "And yes, loads of kangaroos." His clipped British vowels were music to my ears. God, I'd missed him.

The girls erupted into giggles, peppering him with more questions, their words tumbling over one another in their haste to be heard.

I watched, my heart full, as Jamie answered each question with the patience and enthusiasm that made him such a beloved figure in their lives. He might have started as their nanny, but he was the fun uncle now. When it was my turn to get close, I hugged him so hard it was a wonder I didn't break him. I was taller, and where I was all hard and angled, he was softer, slimmer, quieter, with bright-as-a-button blue eyes and the widest smile. I think I lifted him off his feet.

He wriggled. "Bloody hell, you giant," he muttered in my ear. "Get off me!" I let him down, and he thumped my arm. "Guess you all missed me, then?"

I took the cart, and moving it out of the way, used every single one of my muscles. What was in these cases? Bricks?

Back at the car, with the girls in their seats, I opened the trunk and stared at the space and then at the cases. "You're only staying a week, you know," I teased. Jamie was never one to travel light, but six cases, and heavy ones at that?

"Actually, there's a thing," he began, then faltered.

"What is it?" I asked, while struggling to fit the third case into a space it wasn't designed for.

"Your place has a spare room, right?"

I huffed with exertion. "Of course, you don't think I'd make you sleep on the floor!"

"I don't mean that, Oli." He sounded so serious.

For the first time, I properly looked at him, at his nervous expression. "What's wrong?" All kinds of horrific things came to mind—he was ill, he was dying, he was—

"I was hoping it would be okay to stay longer than a week."

I placed a hand on his shoulder. "Of course. You said maybe two weeks, and that's cool with me. The girls will love having you."

He glanced at the last cases on the cart. "How about longer than that? Like, what if I'd finally broken up with Sean-the-asshole because he was cheating on me, and worse, he stole some of my research? And what if, maybe, I was moving to LA for a research project, and I see you and the girls all the time? Get my own place, of course, after a while, but for now—"

I cut him off with another hug. I didn't have any words, just held him close. I couldn't say I was sorry about Sean—Jamie and I may well have kissed once and then fallen about laughing that we were best off staying friends, but that didn't mean I liked whom he'd been dating for the past year. Sean had been a complete waste of space and treated Jamie like shit, so yeah, I was glad he was out of the picture.

Everything fell into place—Jamie was the part of New York I'd missed most, and I needed my friend right now. I could tell him what happened at the clinic and get his support, chat about my nerves about being on the team, and hell, maybe even cover a certain green-eyed cop who took up too much space in my head.

I clapped a hand on his shoulder. "Let's tell the girls their Uncle Jamie is moving in!"

———

IT WAS THREE DAYS LATER, EVERY MUSCLE ACHING FROM practice this morning, when I walked into the clinic's side room. Coach had had me and Ash facing off against Charles, with his wingers, and all three of them, plus damn cones placed all over the rink, meant my legs were doing the jelly thing, totally gassed. I had one meeting here now, and then, I had it in mind that I'd message Jackson again. Maybe get him to meet for coffee somewhere? To ask about the case, obviously.

Who am I kidding? I want to see the man again for a million other reasons.

Like kissing, maybe?

"Morning," I called as I got closer to Lazlo.

"Hey," he murmured, but there was no ready smile, no usual display of pep and cheer.

"You okay?"

He sighed with added drama and spun in his chair a

full three-sixty before facing me again as he scrubbed his eyes.

"Cops were back," he said under his voice, glancing out at the reception area where a small group of adults had gathered in one corner for the next session I was running, plus some other patients in the hard seats. My heart leaped at the idea that Jackson might still be in the building.

"Is he here? I mean, are they here? The cops, I mean… not just the one… both of them…" Wow, way to make things weird, which I clearly had, given Lazlo's expression.

"The detectives left just now."

And somehow, that had made the eternally smiling Lazlo lose his smile?

"Did they find out anything? Do they know who hurt Joe? Oh god, is it Joe? Is he okay?"

"Nope, nope, and Joe's still under." He sighed again. "It's just, I dug out a photo of Joe at his desk and it had the missing picture in it, but it's blurred, and the cops are asking about the picture again with all the people, and I'm stuck going through boxes because the idiot before me never filed anything, and it was so many volunteers, and I can't track half of them down, and I hate the reminder that Joe isn't here to ask." Everything spilled out in a rush, and my heart ached for the kid who I think saw Joe as more of a father figure than a boss. "He's always looking out for us, and we can't do anything."

I thumbed behind me. "You're keeping the place ticking over. That's what you're doing for Joe, and you know how much this place means to him."

He was thoughtful, and then he nodded. "I don't know what else to do."

Heloise came to stand next to us, then leaned over the counter. "Are you okay?" she asked Lazlo, and he nodded. "If you need my help, I can stay after. I'll call my husband and let him know."

She glanced at me, her blue eyes already tearing up, and I caught Lazlo's compassionate gaze.

"It's all good, Heloise, I promise."

She gave us a watery smile, and I frowned after her.

"Maybe we should get her to talk to someone?"

Lazlo nodded. "I'll mention it to Kev—he's the on-call therapist we share with Mercy."

"Cool. And you know if I can help…"

Lazlo shrugged. "It'll be faster if I do it—I know what I'm looking for."

The door opened and a small family with a squalling baby came in and headed straight for the front desk. Lazlo smiled then, and no one would realize the smile wasn't wholly real.

"Welcome. How can I help?" he asked.

I backed away and headed into the small conference room with its oval table and ten chairs rammed around it. It was a plain space with a whiteboard and some medical posters on the wall. Two sets of parents were already in there, looking tired, but attentive. Nurse Maggie was ready to talk serious medical routines, and I was tagged in.

"Hi, everyone," I waved and took a seat near Maggie.

Everyone said a hello, and I could immediately tell one of the dads knew who I was when he mumbled something to the guy sitting next to him, then sneered at me.

Hell, I was used to that.

"This is Oliver," Maggie carried on. "He'll be talking about the practical uses of the glucose monitor."

I lifted my sleeve, showing them the device in my arm. "This is a CGM, continuous glucose monitor," I began, then lifted one out of a box in front of me to demonstrate. "It's not a big thing, but it can alert you to low sugars while your children are sleeping."

The moms listened, nodding slowly, taking it all in. The dads, though, they were a tougher crowd, their faces etched with a mix of skepticism and something like frustration.

One of the dads, the same one who'd recognized me, a broad-shouldered guy with tired eyes, cut me off. "Is this just a one-day charity thing you do to feel good about yourself, Mr. Hockey Star? My daughter is two! She's a baby, and you're sitting there telling us it's just a tiny thing when we know it's not! You don't know shit!" There was an edge to his voice, a challenge.

Before I could respond, Maggie gave him a sharp glare. "Steve," she hissed, a clear warning in her voice.

I got it, though. It was hard to accept that your kid had a lifelong condition; it could make anyone lash out.

"I don't know your daughter, sir," I replied, keeping eye contact, "but I'm here because I know what it's like. I've known the three a.m. scares and the hospital trips. This," I said, holding up the monitor, "could make a real difference for your children, if you try it."

The room was silent for a moment, the lone sound the hum of the overhead lights. Steve relaxed a bit. The nurse jumped in to explain the daily insulin routines, and I sat down with the families to talk more about living with diabetes. It wasn't just about dropping in as a sports figure; it was personal. I was there to help because I understood what they were facing, and maybe could make their lives easier if they needed financial support.

Not that they'd know the last bit, but still, I was giving back the best way I knew.

"Mr. Cowan?"

Steve was the last person out of the room, and I got the sense he wanted to talk to me.

"Hi?" I waited to see what came next. Sometimes, a person never saw the bits of me that weren't hockey, but I always lived in hope.

"I…" He offered a hand. "I'm sorry for my outburst."

"It's all good," I said and shook his hand warmly.

"I'm on my own, you know, my wife… she's gone, and it's just me, and I feel so overwhelmed, and I don't know what to do."

"I have an hour; would you like to chat in here? Or get a coffee?"

His eyes widened. "You'd do that?"

I clapped him on the shoulder. "Of course. Let's go."

This is what I did best, a beast in the game, but understanding and kind when I was off the ice.

My only regret? That I never got to ask *Jackson* to meet for coffee.

Chapter Eight

Jackson

A WEEK HAD PASSED SINCE THE INCIDENT AT THE CLINIC, and we were no closer to finding the jerk who'd done it than we had been on day one. You'd think that with so many witnesses to a crime, we'd have been right on that guy's doorstep within hours. Sadly, we lived in a huge city with a massive criminal element that made people disappear faster than new iPhones. Mack and I were running out of options and avenues, but we weren't giving up. Joe was still in an induced coma, so there was no information coming from the victim. We'd tracked down everyone in the missing photo, ran background checks, and confirmed alibis, leaving us with nothing but a list of selfless medical professionals trying to help the poor and indigent in this huge stewpot of glitz and poverty we called Los Angeles.

Oliver had touched base a few times to tug my chain about the lack of results, and a call came through when I was sitting in court testifying in a case against one Randolph Piscotty, a mid-tier racketeer that the DA and my department had been stiff as a fence post to nab. And we had. Granted it was on tax evasion, but hey, we'd pulled him off the streets. Which had opened up a bit of a tussle for power, ending with four dead Piscotty underlings discovered stacked like cordwood in an alley in Pacific Palisades. Since they were linked to the Piscotty crime family, homicide pulled us in to take a peek. It was about as you would think. Four corpses baking in the warm California sun. Just another day in the life.

So yeah, I'd been in court the last time Oliver had jangled my nerves. I'd let the call go to voicemail as the judge was glowering at me from on high. She hated cell phones in her courtroom, even if they were in your pocket. The woman had ears like a bat, and the vibration of a cell phone was like the whine of mosquito wings. I got the look, a warning about my phone, and a sniping little dissertation during the lunch break from the district attorney.

Oliver got a snide little message in return as I stuffed a taco from a truck parked a block from the courthouse in my mouth. Mack rolled his eyes as he wolfed down a burrito. The hockey player replied ten minutes later with a softly worded apology, citing his distress over his friend as the reason he kept poking me. So, being the dear heart that I am, I texted him back saying I understood, and that we were doing all we could. And then I added, because his dark eyes had been haunting me since our lunch at the steakhouse, that if I thought of anything else, I would contact him.

Hopefully, the vision of his eyes and those damned kissable lips would ease up soon. I'd worked my dick pretty hard the past few nights while old episodes of *Kojak* played in the background. Jerking off to the fantasy of a witness to a pretty ugly crime sucking your cock surely had to be against departmental guidelines for proper cop behavior. My brain knew that, but my prick had not gotten the memo. I'd not felt a pull to a man like this in... forever. It freaked me out, yet I couldn't clear him from my head.

———

TWO DAYS LATER, I FOUND MYSELF STARING DOWN AT A plate of spaghetti with meatballs that my ex-brother-in-law and his son, my favorite nephew in the world, had cooked for me. Leo was out for a visit as part of the custody agreement between Bryce and my sister. Bryce and his boyfriend—the ex-hockey player for the Storm, Michael Zhang—and Leo were chatting away at the dining room table in the house where Bryce and Mike now lived. Nice place with a small yard in Glendale from where both men could commute to work.

"Uncle Jack, I helped make the meatballs," Leo informed me as a bowl of salad was forced into my hands. Bryce smiled in that hippie goody-goody way of his, but his expression was firm. "And the salad. I picked the lettuce and tomato from the garden. The cucumber, too. You should eat some. Dad says fresh greens make you smile more."

I threw Bryce a look. "I smile plenty," I replied, then grinned broadly at everyone around the table. Michael snorted in amusement. I liked the guy. He was good for

Bryce, and vice versa. They seemed happy as hell. "I just have a lettuce-swallowing reflex ailment that makes me gag anytime lettuce slides down my throat. It's really a curse. The last guy I—"

"Okay, so no salad for Uncle Jack." Bryce glared at me as he swept the salad bowl away. Mission accomplished. "Why don't you tell Uncle Jack your big news?"

"Oh yeah!" Leo nearly burst from his seat. He had so much energy. Christ, I missed being ten years old and filled with all that effervescence. I moved through my days like a zombie, all the joy of life slowly sapped from me by my job. It was hard to be perky when the first thing you did in the morning was kneel beside a body stashed behind a dumpster. No wonder so many cops were on anti-depressants. "Mom said I could spend the whole summer out here next season, so I can attend the hockey camps that the Storm sponsors. I'm getting really good."

He was. I went to all the games I could where he played. It was a juggling act since Leo lived out of state, but his father and my sister somehow made it work.

"That's really cool," I said and found that I meant it. I'd spent mostly every Saturday at the local rink watching Leo play. Of course, the sight of Oliver coming in to volunteer on occasion was a bonus. "So, the Storm. Are they doing okay?"

Mike blinked at my question. I wasn't known for my hockey love. I was more a football and basketball guy, but since the family was now part of the team, albeit in a distanced manner, it seemed prudent to show more backing for the sport.

"They're doing well," Michael replied, his gaze

flicking to Bryce, who shrugged, then passed me a container of grated cheese. "Cowboy has been a nice addition. Brings that old-school flavor to the team that was missing. Big beefy guy, plays with an edge, always ready to jump into a tilt."

I nodded, as if I knew what the fuck he was talking about. Edging in my mind had nothing to do with skates and pucks…

"Oliver. Yeah, that's nice. He seems pretty okay." I twirled some red strands of pasta around my fork. Everyone grunted in agreement. Shit. Now where did I go with this conversation? *Think, Winwood. You're an expert interrogator. Just ask what you want to ask in a roundabout way so as not to arouse suspicion.* "I heard that he was a widower."

"Yes, sadly, he lost his wife to cancer a couple of years ago," Michael said before passing a basket of warm breadsticks to me. "He and the girls are doing as well as can be expected. My brother and Clare are helping with the kids when they can. I think Charles said that a new nanny had arrived from New York to ease his burden. Must be hard having to balance hockey with kids when you're alone."

"Mm, must be," I mumbled around my spaghetti. The sauce was a little bland, but I'd not had a home-cooked meal since the last time I'd visited my sister, so I was not going to bitch.

I let the conversation drift to other things, less sad things for Leo to hear, and ate myself into a carb coma. I hugged my nephew goodbye an hour later, shook hands with Bryce and Mike, and slugged my way to my Riviera.

The old gal was the prettiest thing I owned. A classic 1973 boat-tailed hunter-green vixen I'd found at an auction and had spent far too much on. Worth every penny, though. They didn't make cars like these anymore. I'd worry about retirement later.

"Hey, Ramona," I said as I sat behind the wheel and stretched out my legs. Yes, leg room aplenty, as well as a working ashtray and lighter. Neither of which I was using, as I was back on the patches. For Leo. I'd gain forty pounds if tonight's meal was any indication. Oral fixations, Mack would say, could be curbed by putting something other than a cigarette into your mouth. My first thought was a big fat cock belonging to a slightly older, but sinfully sexy, hockey player. Mack probably meant a stick of Juicy Fruit or a Life Saver. "Okay, baby, let's take a drive."

The .455 cubic inch V-8 roared to life. I nearly came in my pants. Taking note of the local speed laws, Ramona and I cruised. It was close to midnight. I really did not want to go home. My dingy place would seem even dingier after spending the night with Bryce and his nice little family. My dead orchid was not much of a conversationalist. Not that I wanted someone to talk to or anything like that. Sitting around a table with food, laughing and sharing the day's happenings was for those who didn't investigate crimes for a living.

Seems to work okay for Mack and all the other married cops. Just saying.

"No, no, that's… okay, yes, I guess it did, but how?" I asked as we pulled to a red light and chilled. The streets were always busy, but traffic was lighter now. A blue sedan eased up on my left to wait for the light. "What do they talk about? We can't discuss our work. What the fuck do you say to someone who lives in the uncorrupted world? How do you have a discussion over a frozen pot pie with a normal person because let's be honest here, my job ain't exactly dinner-fare-talk-friendly. Oh yeah, and by the way, sugar plum, remember that embezzler who tried to wheedle a few million from a local bank? He shot himself in front of his wife and kids. Can you pass the salt?"

I glanced over to see a couple staring at me as if I were a lunatic.

"Go about your business. Nothing to see here," I told them as the light changed. They took off to put some space between them and me. No one really understood the finer aspects of talking to yourself. I cranked up the radio— finding a classic station that played only 50s, 60s and 70s because Ramona liked those decades—and let the lovely voice of Toni Tenille guide me through the maze of city streets.

We drove and drove, passing through tough neighborhoods, then through some pretty swanky ones. I pulled into a gas station to fill up my car. Those .455 engines were gas-guzzlers. As I was idling away at the gas pump, hose in my hand, Ramona sucking down the unleaded—she had had the valve guides, valves, and ignition work done to run smoothly on unleaded—like the thirsty harlot that she was, my phone buzzed in my back pocket. I sighed wearily. It was one thing to be cruising the city because you loathed the idea of going home. It was quite another to get pinged with something that could be work-related at this hour.

When the pump kicked off, I eased the nozzle out, placed it back in the holder, and removed my phone from my pocket. Oh. Oh, okay, well, that was a nice note. Seemed the swelling in Joe Baxter's skull had lessened. He was now awake, sore and battered, but able and most willing to speak to the police. Tomorrow. I thought about texting Oliver Cowan, but instead opted to pass by his place. It was only ten minutes from where I was now. I didn't want to look too closely at how I'd mindlessly driven to the edges of Oliver's neighborhood. Better to not put a spotlight on that. With Lionel Richie flowing out of the windows, I crept into the upper-class neighborhood Oliver called home. His rental was a big place, huge in comparison to my crappy apartment, and a few lights shone through the windows of the first floor.

I parked in the street, cut the engine, and ran my fingers through my hair.

This is stupid. Why are we even here? Why not just text the man?

I couldn't argue with myself. This *was* stupid. But my sandaled feet were carrying me to his front door just the same. There were flowers in a pot on the front porch, as well as a pair of tiny pink sneakers that appeared to be soaking wet. I rapped on the door softly, unwilling to ring the bell and wake the whole house.

This is beyond stupid. Jackson, what are you doing here? This is not cool. If Franks hears that you showed up at a witness's house at midnight to—

The door opened. I stared into a pair of pretty,

masculine eyes that were not Oliver Cowan's. The guy was fucking gorgeous. Short dark hair, tidy scruff, glasses, lean and wearing a silky shirt. Holding a cup of tea. I knew it was tea because the mug said so. *Tea Time* it read.

"Yes, can I help you?" he asked in a posh British Hugh Grant type accent.

I literally took a step back to double check the numbers beside the front door. Yep, I was at the right house.

Rattled beyond belief, I fell back on what I knew best. I removed my badge from my belt and held it up in front of his stupidly good-looking face. "Detective Jackson Winwood, LAPD Organized Crimes Division. I'd like to speak to Oliver Cowan if he's here?"

Whoever he was examined my badge closely, then glanced at me a few dozen times. When he was convinced it was my face on the card, he nodded. Only once.

"Oh, Ollie, yes, of course he's here. Come in, Officer." Mr. Brit stepped back, letting me ease into the foyer. "We're just having a cup of tea before we head to bed. Can I fetch you some, Detective?"

Bed? They were heading to bed? Together. Fuck. So my sexy hockey player *was* taken.

"No, thanks. I'm more of a coffee drinker." I wished like hell I had my Minnie thermos. I also wished like hell I'd not done this. I'd been perfectly happy tugging off to my personal fantasy of me and Oliver being all over each other. Now, I was faced with the reality that Oliver had this man in his life and home. It was a slap in the face. "Are you and Mr. Cowan uhm…?"

Pretty Boy gasped, then chuckled. "Bloody hell, no; I'm a friend of the family."

Uh-huh. He seemed quite at home here, with his shirt unbuttoned and his hair ruffled. I still thought maybe he and Oliver had been playing hide the crumpet when I knocked. Fucker.

Wait. What? Whoa!

I scowled at the tea-sipper, trying to clear the unwarranted dislike from my brain, when Oliver appeared in a doorway to the left of us. Seeing the man in lounge clothes made my lungs seize up. Christ, he was beautiful.

"Detective Winwood, is there something wrong?" Oliver asked, stepping up to stand beside the guy with the tea mug, who was eyeballing me over the top of his spectacles with interest. "Did you get a break in the case?"

"No, not yet, but the hospital just called to let me know that Mr. Baxter is now conscious and speaking to family and friends."

Oliver exhaled in relief. Tea Sipper gave him a hug. It took all I had to not unholster my gun and conk the Brit right between the eyes. It would be quick. Relatively painless. And would get his perfectly manicured hands off Oliver.

"That's amazing news. Thank you for coming all the way over to let us know. You could have texted," Oliver said.

Tea Man smiled warmly at Oliver.

Yep, one *smack* with the butt of my gun. Out cold. Him and his tea. Americans drank coffee, damn it. We dumped tea into harbors. One if by land, two if by sea and all of that. They both stared at me, waiting for a reply. Shit.

"It's all part of the LAPD's commitment to offering witnesses every available courtesy."

"Oh, that's lovely," the Brit commented.

"I know, also, if you want, I can pick you up tomorrow morning to go visit Mr. Baxter as, yet, another part of that witness courtesy we spoke of just a minute ago." I spewed out, then winced as the words hit my ear holes.

What the fuck? What the ever-loving fuck? Since when do we play chauffeur?

"No need for that. I'm sure I can manage on my own. Thank you for dropping by, Detective. Sorry for annoying you for the past week. I've been kind of worried about Joe and the whole investigation. That, on top of the move, and the girls, and our schedule has just been... well, it's been a lot." Oliver ran his hand through his hair. It looked fluffy.

Fluffy. Holy shit, Jackson, back out of this situation now.

"Understandable," I croaked and began moving backwards toward the door. Fluffy. Fuck's sake. "No harm, no foul. It's been a traumatic experience for you. No need to apologize. Thank you for your time. Sorry to show up so late. Have a good night."

I nearly fell out of the open door in my haste to get some distance between me, Mr. Brit, and Oliver Fluffy Hair. It was times like this I wished Ramona had computerized components so I could command her to run my stupid ass over.

Fluffy hair. FFS.

Chapter Nine

Oliver

I watched Detective Winwood—Jackson's—retreat, his departure as abrupt as his arrival. There was something about the way he moved—a confident, albeit slightly flustered, stride—that caught my attention more than I cared to admit. The door clicked shut, and the space between us suddenly felt too vast.

Jamie nudged me, a knowing smirk dancing on his lips. "Someone's got a thing for the sexy cop, huh?"

I rolled my eyes, feeling heat rise to my cheeks despite the coolness of the evening. "What are we, twelve?" I shot back, trying to deflect with humor, though Jamie's grin only broadened.

"Come off it, Ollie. You should've seen your face when he mentioned 'witness courtesy,'" Jamie quipped, making quote gestures with his fingers.

"Shut it, Jamie," I said, the warmth in my face now undoubtedly a telltale blush. I knew there was no use arguing; Jamie's teasing had hit its mark. Detective

Winwood was… compelling, in a way I hadn't expected and wasn't sure what to do with.

Jamie clapped me on the shoulder, his laughter filling the room, a sound I'd normally welcome, but right now, I was all over the freaking place. Attraction for Jackson, irritability at Jamie, and it was that strange itch of irritation that had me checking my watch. My sugar levels were okay, so maybe it was just plain old me being an irritable asshole.

"I just don't know what to think," I said.

Jamie's laughter faded into a softer, more serious tone as he caught the hesitation in my voice. He leaned against the wall, his expression turning thoughtful. "But seriously, mate, it's been what, two years since…" His voice trailed off, respecting the silence that wrapped around my wife's memory.

I let out a sigh, running a hand through my hair. "Yeah, two years," I murmured. I could feel the weight of the time passed, each day a balancing act between being a father, a professional athlete, and just… me—all while managing my health.

"And you haven't thought about dating again?" Jamie's question was gentle, treading lightly on a topic we rarely broached.

I shook my head, the image of the detective flashing in my mind, uninvited, but not unwelcome. "I don't know, Jamie. It's not just me I have to think about. There's Daisy and Scarlett."

Jamie nodded. "They want you to be happy, you know. They've said as much to Clare."

"Clare?" I was confused.

"You know, Clare, married to your team captain?"

"I know who Clare is. I just didn't know you talked to her."

"We both do school pickups, of course I talk to Clare. I've even talked to Charles, and he's kinda cute." Jamie wrinkled his nose. "In a wholly straight and married way."

I glanced up, surprised. "And the kids have talked to her?"

"Yes," Jamie confirmed. "Kids are perceptive. They have to know you've been lonely."

A moment passed as I considered his words, the truth of them sinking in deep. "But what if I'm not ready? What if I never am?"

"That's okay too," Jamie said, his voice steady. "But don't close yourself off because you're afraid. You deserve happiness, Oliver. So do the girls."

"But a man?"

"They don't have any trouble with Charlie's brother, who is dating another guy."

"But Michael isn't their dad."

The idea of moving on, of finding someone new, felt like trying to navigate without a compass. But, as Jamie's words echoed in the quiet room, I couldn't ignore the small spark of possibility flickering within me—a sign that maybe, just maybe, it was time to start exploring life beyond the roles I'd grown so accustomed to, and maybe that exploration could start with the first person I'd felt attracted to since Melissa passed. She'd made me promise to find someone to make me happy. Hell, even as I held her, and she took her last breath, she told me to be happy.

How could I do what she asked?

"Thanks, Jamie," I finally said. "I'll think about it. In the meantime, I need to focus on finding someone to be here for the girls permanently when you leave. I can't expect you to stay here with them forever."

"What if I wanted to?" Jamie asked with caution.

My chest tightened. Was he saying he wanted to be with me? And maybe not as his best friend? "We tried kissing and—"

He thumped me in the chest. "Jesus, mate, I don't mean us as partners. I mean, me finding a place close by and covering things you can't do. My research is flexible, and I love the girls, and I love your face, too, you big stupid Yank."

I shoved him back. "The girls love you. I can tolerate you."

He grinned at me, then pushed off from the wall, clapping a hand on my shoulder as he passed. "Whatever you decide about Cop McSexy, I'm here for you. And hey, if you ever want to talk about… sexy cops or anything else, you know where to find me."

I cracked a smile, the tension easing from my shoulders. "I'll keep that in mind."

He headed for bed and left me alone with the quiet hum of the house and the girls fast asleep. I found myself reaching for my phone, the weight of the day pushing me to seek some sort of connection, however brief it might be. This was so wrong. This was stupid. I bet Jackson wasn't visiting tonight as anything *but* a courtesy, and here I was reading something into it.

I tapped out a message, the screen's glow bright in the dim room.

> Oliver: Hey, Detective, it's Oliver. Just wanted to say thanks again for the update earlier.

Now what? That wasn't a message that left any room for discussion.

> Oliver: If you ever want tickets to a game, I can hook you up.

The reply came quicker than I expected.

> Jackson: Appreciate the offer, but I'm not much of a hockey fan.

Well shit. That was clearly not the way I wanted this to go. I was supposed to give him an opening, get him to a game, treat him to dinner, have sex.

The fuck? I shook my head to clear that particular thought process. Okay, I needed to pivot. Tease. *I can do this. I have game.*

> Oliver: Next, you'll tell me you don't like sunshine and beaches either.

There was a brief pause before Jackson's response popped up.

> Jackson: I might not watch a lot of hockey, but I'd watch you anytime, on the ice or off.

Wow, that man had way more game than me. He'd actually come out and full-on flirted. I stared at the message, a mix of surprise and something that felt suspiciously like excitement bubbling up inside me. This was new territory, and fuck, what did I do now? The last time I'd flirted properly had been with Melissa, and I'd been seventeen, for God's sake.

> Oliver: Is that so? Well, maybe I'll have to give you a reason to come to a game then. I promise it's more exciting than it looks on TV.

Great, there was absolutely zero game in that. I mean, what even was the connection there? All I'd done was mention the game again.

> Jackson: With you on the ice? I'm there.
>
> Jackson: I'll even have one of those signs up for you.
>
> Oliver: What will it say?
>
> Jackson: Come score on me.
>
> Jackson: emphasis on come

YEP, THAT WOULD DO IT. JESUS, I WAS HARD AS STEEL. Jackson was winning the flirting with a solid gold medal performance. The conversation was veering into uncharted waters for me, and though part of me wanted to retreat to safer topics, another part was curious to see where this would go. Jamie had said it was okay. The kids didn't want me to be lonely. I was attracted to Jackson.

Come on Team!Oliver.

Oliver: Tell you what, how about I leave a
ticket for you at will call next game? No
pressure.

*Oh Jesus, what the fuck was that? Why didn't I make
more of the come part? I could have written anything
about wanting to come, and instead I did* that?

Jackson: I'll make the sign.

Oliver: I'll look for it.

Jackson: Goodnight, Mr. Hockey.

Oliver: Goodnight, Detective.

I put the phone down, a small, uncertain smile tugging
at my lips. Maybe Jamie *was* right; perhaps it was time to
start exploring what life had to offer beyond the rink and
my responsibilities. Tonight's exchange with Jackson was
just talking, just words on a screen, but it felt like a first,
tentative step toward something new.

Something possible.

I STRODE INTO THE HOSPITAL ROOM WHERE JOE LAY. THE
sight of him—pale and fragile against the white sheets—
squeezed my heart tight. He was asleep when I first got
there, and his sister, sitting by his side, rose to shake my
hand. As if she'd already said it a hundred times she
explained what his injuries were in simple language.

He'd suffered a subdural hematoma, a severe brain

injury, and it was this that had left him comatose for the last few days. He had memory issues, but he was resting peacefully.

I thanked her, and she took the opportunity to grab coffees. I sat in the other chair, the monitors beeping a steady, reassuring rhythm.

His eyes flickered open, and he stared at the ceiling.

"Hey, Joe," I said as I stood and tried not to loom and overwhelm him.

His eyes fluttered closed, and then open, and a weak, but genuine, smile spread across his face. "Oliver… you came."

"Wouldn't be anywhere else," I assured him, pulling the chair closer to the bed. His sister came back at that moment and shut the door behind her.

"Brought you a coffee," she said to me and handed it over, along with a handful of creamers and sugar. "Not that the sugar will help. The coffee is rank."

"Thank you. Joe's awake."

Her wry smile over the coffee softened, and she pressed a kiss to her brother's head. "Hey, big bro," she whispered.

He caught her hand. "Gemma…" he began, then blinked at me, and back at her.

"It's okay. Oliver's here."

Joe's gaze was unfocused, his words slurred. "Cops… here… questions," he mumbled, struggling to piece the sentence together. "I got retro—ret—gr—nesia—"

"Retrograde amnesia," his sister interjected smoothly when Joe tripped over the words. "He doesn't remember a thing after getting a drink and sitting at his desk." She paused a moment, then swallowed. "They say he might not get those memories back, but it's common with head injuries."

I could see the frustration clouding Joe's eyes and the corresponding fear in Gemma's.

"Yeah, retro… retrograde," Joe attempted again, the effort furrowing his brow.

"It's okay, sweetie," Gemma soothed, placing a reassuring hand on his. "You just focus on getting better. I'll talk to Oliver."

"M'okay," Joe whispered and closed his eyes again.

"Doc said it was like trying to watch a TV with a bad signal. The pictures might be there, but they'd be flickering, out of focus and out of reach. I'm not sure I want him to recall a damn thing."

The worry lines around Gemma's eyes spoke of sleepless nights and fear. She leaned forward, her voice hushed as if the walls themselves might be eavesdropping.

"I get that," I commiserated. I didn't want to remember the attack, and all I'd done was observe the aftermath.

"Can you tell me what happened?" she asked, her gaze fixed on me.

I took a deep breath, recalling the event as best I could. "I remember walking into Joe's office with the intention to cheer him up," I began, my gaze flickering to Joe, who seemed to be following along as best as he could. "He was at his desk, and… that's when I saw the gunman."

Gemma leaned in closer, her hand gripping Joe's. "And what happened then?"

"Umm, he was panicked, erratic. He'd hit Joe here." I touched my temple. "And he had a gun pointed at Joe, and

I froze, not wanting to provoke him. I knew I needed to talk him down, to de-escalate the situation," I explained, the scene replaying behind my eyes like a film I couldn't pause.

"And then?" Her voice was steady, but her eyes brimmed with unshed tears.

"I didn't get a chance to stop it. He turned the gun on me, but all I had in my hands were coffee and files. I couldn't... I couldn't do anything," I admitted, the helplessness of the moment washing over me once more. "Before I could even think, the man took off. I went straight to Joe before he fell to the ground. Called 911 immediately after," I finished, feeling a shiver despite the room's warmth. I left out the attacker's threat, and finding Heloise locked in the janitor's closet—I'm not sure she needed to hear the nitty-gritty.

Gemma's eyes were bright, and her shoulders slumped. "Thank you for being there with him," she whispered, squeezing her brother's hand.

I offered a small, reassuring smile, wishing there was more I could have done, more I could do now. "I just wish I knew the attacker, or something that could help catch whoever did this to Joe."

"The detectives keep asking him about a photo on the wall, but he's confused. I'm not stupid, and I looked the detectives up; they work organized crime. I don't understand. Joe would never have anything to do with that."

By the time I left, Joe had woken a couple of times, and we'd even joked about the color of Lazlo's hair, which was a running theme.

It felt almost normal.

But I was a mess, tired, still three hours away from picking the girls up from their after-school club, and although I loved that the girls were happy in their new school, I felt at loose ends.

Bewildered by all the thoughts running through my head.

I exited the hospital, my mind still partly with Joe and Gemma, but as I made my way to the parking lot, a familiar figure caught my eye. There was Jackson, standing near my bike, looking every bit the detective off-duty, yet undeniably himself.

He seemed lost in thought, his gaze fixed on my Ducati. It wasn't until I was close enough that he shook off his reverie, the corners of his mouth lifting slightly. "Hey," he said, his voice casual, but his eyes betraying a hint of intent. "Was just visiting a witness from another case and saw your bike. Thought I'd hover for a bit, see if you were around."

The sheltered bike bay felt like a world away from the rest of the hospital. It was quieter, more intimate, a private meeting place for us.

Or was that only my wishful thinking of what I'd love to happen right here, in front of my bike, over my bike? Fuck. Against the wall.

I leaned against the bike, crossing my arms. "You recognize it, huh?" I replied, feeling a mixture of pride and curiosity.

Jackson took a step closer, his eyes still on the bike, but clearly not talking about the machinery. "Hard to miss. It stands out, just like its owner," he said, his voice low.

The tension between us was crazy, a current buzzing in the quiet space of the parking bay. And before I could think of anything else to say, anything clever or witty, Jackson closed the distance between us.

His lips met mine in a deep, confident kiss. It was as if all the questions simmering beneath the surface found their answers in that contact. There was no hesitation, no doubt, just the shared understanding that this was right—perfect, even.

My hands found their way to his waist, pulling him closer as I surrendered to the kiss. Every bit of uncertainty about life, about moving on, about taking risks—it all melted away. At that moment, it was only Jackson and me.

When we finally parted, the look we shared spoke volumes.

"I needed to do that," Jackson murmured.

I reached up and cradled his face, loving that he had extra height on me, loving that I had to lean back to gaze up at him. I wondered what he'd be like in bed—was he growly and grumpy, would he order me around, would he make me come like I'd never done with a man before?

"I'm glad you did," I whispered back.

The slamming of a car door echoed from the parking lot, but it was enough to startle us both.

"I have to go," he said and stole one more kiss before turning smartly on his heels and leaving.

Taking his sexy self away from me before I jumped his bones in public.

Probably a good call.

Chapter Ten

Jackson

Sleep was nonexistent.

No matter how I tried, or how many glasses of Wild Turkey I poured myself, my eyes were not closing. That kiss. Jesus, Mary, and Ralph. What a kiss. I could still feel the tingling on my lips. Or maybe that was the whiskey. After a couple of shots, I rose from my sofa, gathered up the booze and my dead orchid, and went out onto the patio. The sounds of the inner city met me as I plunked my ass down on cold concrete. I had no furniture out here. Why would I invest in a patio set when the view consisted of the back of another apartment building? Also, people who had little tables with umbrellas, matching chairs, and flowering things in ceramic pots were like Oliver. Who had a house, and flowers, and kids, and a live-in friend, who I still didn't think was trustworthy.

I'd see if I could touch base with Interpol tomorrow. No, that would be today. Christ. I sipped my warm whiskey, the orchid resting between my legs.

"I'm sorry I let you die," I whispered to the flower as it

sat there. "If it's any consolation, I tend to let most things in my life wither and die. I don't know why." I took another sip, then reached into my front pocket for a cigarette. Only there were none. I was quitting. Again. Motherfucker. I tore off the patch on my biceps, got to my feet, and did the hunt of shame. Anyone who has tried to quit smoking knows the hunt of shame. It's where you rummage and toss your house in search of a cigarette. I found none between couch cushions or in jacket pockets. So, I sunk lower and pawed in the trash in hopes my housekeeper hadn't dumped it. She had. So not one stale butt was to be found.

"Motherfucker," I repeated just because it felt good, then went to find another patch. After that was stuck on, I returned to the patio and my lonely orchid, and proceeded to drink myself into a state of misery. Thankfully, I did doze off, but my phone alarm had me up at seven. My ass was numb, my head felt like a rhino had sat on it, and my mental state was still a wreck. I got to my feet with a moan, carried the empty bottle and dead orchid back inside, and showered.

Mack had court today. That left me on my own to sort out a shit-ton of paperwork and touch base on the slew of cases we were buried under. The county could not get new blood in this unit fast enough to suit me. I'd stopped on the way to the precinct for coffee and two slices of breakfast pizza after filling up my Buick. I'd not stopped thinking of Oliver's lips and the way he had felt pressed against me since our mouths had parted.

I had kissed a lot of men in my twenty-eight years. None of those lip-to-lip meetings had dug into my soul like tasting Oliver Cowan had. Even now, several hours later, my body was humming with residual lust. Not a good thing, as I had case files up the ass. So, shoving a certain sexy hockey player out of my mind—or trying to—I got back to work and checked the internal server to see what had come to the top of the cesspool overnight. I had a shitty system for organizing tasks. There were three categories. Super Important Shit or SIS. Medium Important Shit or MIS. And Not Important Shit or NIS. One of the cops I had partnered with before I'd gotten my detective badge had taught me that system. Barclay Pressman. Good man. Good cop. Dead now. Shot while investigating a noise complaint. Left a wife and three boys. I'd attended far too many funerals for law enforcement officers in my time on the force. And sadly, there would be a lot more before they gave me a gold watch. Given I chased down and incarcerated the mob, Mexican cartels, and feral street gangs, I'd probably be in the ground way before I got that Timex.

Nothing that had my name on it, nor had anything to do with any of my active cases. I started working on follow-ups on the guy we'd found behind the dumpster a few weeks ago. Seemed he had been traced back to one of the lower echelon pushers on the east side. The only odd thing about the shooting was that it wasn't your typical gangland execution. This guy had been carved up in a particular fashion that had deranged monster written all over it. Homicide was working that one, so I closed it out after touching base with Paul "Peanut" Williams—Peanut due to the small size of his head—and moved onto more mundane tasks, such as gathering admissible evidence, making phone calls, and other things that did little to keep my pickled brain from drifting.

With my partner in court for the day, I knew I should keep my ass in my chair, but this office, this building, was growing cramped. I needed some air. Somewhere clean. Somewhere I could sort through the mess inside my skull. Somewhere calm and peaceful. Maybe the beach. Cap would totally buy that I felt sick. I looked like death warmed over. Yeah, some time on the sand with the sun on my face and my toes in the surf would do me wonders.

"Hey, Mary, get your face on. We have a pornography raid to back up. Warrant just came in, and SAFE needs some bodies," Berke called as he and his partner bustled ass through our section of desks and water coolers. Mary. Nice. Whatever. I'd been called worse, for sure, but one day, Paul Berke and I were going to have a long talk about suitable nicknames. All cops had them. Berke was known as Drippy due to his constant allergies and Mason was called Joker because he appeared a great deal like Cesar Julio Romero Jr. from the 60s *Batman* show. Mack was Kilt because he was Scottish, and me, I was Mary because I was gay and Berke was a jerkoff old homophobe. All the other guys called me Rollo when it suited. It was some stupid sling-around to my last name being Winwood and the singer Steve Winwood having a hit song about rolling with it. Yeah, I never said cops were good at nicknames— we just had them.

"Face is already on. This is as pretty as I get, Drippy," I barked, knowing this raid would probably be on child porn producers that SAFE had been investigating. Nothing said "good morning world, it's a fine day," better than bringing down the hammer on sickos who preyed on kids. The flip side to that perky day arresting scumbags was that many times the kids were on site, sometimes held against their will. Lots of children of color went missing every day. The stats were horrific, and while all of us in law enforcement did our best, sex trafficking was alive and well and tied into many other things. Such as my division of organized crime.

Yeah, the job had its up and downs for sure.

I tossed down the last dregs of coffee in my Minnie thermos and went to play with the boys from Sexual Assault and Felony Enforcement. Generally, our little bands didn't share the sandbox, but given how low every department was on able-bodied cops, we pulled together when necessary. Mack was going to be peeved to miss out on all the fun, but as much as we bitched about court dates, that was what we did all of this for. Hopefully, all the hard work, cold beds, and empty whiskey bottles resulted in getting bad guys off the streets.

We geared up for the raid, pulling on Kevlar raid vests in case things got dicey. Typically, the "breach" team pulled on the most gear. As the detectives who were serving as backups for SAFE, we were there to help lock down the scene after the breach unit entered, secured the site, and deemed it safe for us to enter.

Not as exciting as it was on TV, but still better than sitting in the office dwelling on a wet lip-lock with a witness. A witness I wanted to toss over the nearest counter and fuck seventeen ways to Sunday. It was all so bad, on so many fronts, but there it was. So yeah, this would be a nice distraction. We piled into an unmarked car that Conrad "Chip" Cooley from SAFE drove, and made our way to the outskirts of LA, to a small run-down building at the end of a strip mall. Next to a nail salon called Wins Nails sat Honeybee Video Productions.

There were five detectives on-site, along with a small breach team of about six SWAT members. As I said, we were there for the ice cream—the breaching unit did all the hard work. Still, things could escalate quickly, so backup was always appreciated.

We lingered a bit, just a moment or two, using the windowless brick wall as a buffer as SWAT did their thing. Shouting as they busted into the front of the video production store. Flash bangs went off and at least fifteen men erupted out of the rear of the nail salon, as well as the video store. We all gave chase as soon as we locked eyes. Feminine screams could be heard from the interior of the nail parlor along with the loud shouts of the breach unit. I locked my sights on a tall Black male, with white hair, blue shirt, cargo shorts, and new Nike high tops. Someone behind me called my name. Well, they called Mary, which I chose to ignore as adrenaline raced through me.

Cops erupted out of the rear of several stores and ran hard.

White Hair glanced back at me once. His eyes widened, and then, he sped up. The fucker. Maybe the whole smoking cessation thing was a good idea if this was what I was doing on occasion. Wheezing slightly, I nonetheless maintained distance even if I didn't overtake him. I switched on my body cam and he led me on a fucking merry chase, zipping around parked cars, into a four-lane road where we both nearly got mowed down, and into a playground. Over a rusty fence he went, landing awkwardly, his left leg buckling for a split second. Pushing myself to my limits—fucking greasy food and menthol smokes had to go—I arced over the fence, one hand on the top rail, and landed on my feet. Women and kids screamed. Ten or so guys shooting hoops stopped the game instantly. A basketball bounced once, twice, and thrice on the old court as I lunged at the man who was getting to his fancy Nikes. I took him down with a football tackle I had learned back in my high school days playing defensive tackle for the Milford Mustangs. Go Mustangs!

We skidded over the cracked blacktop of the basketball court, him throwing wild haymakers at my head. One landed solidly in my eye.

"Motherfucker," I spat out in pain as tears ran down my right cheek. I pinned him down, knees on his arms, as my overworked lungs sucked in as much air as they could. "You have the… right to… remain silent…" I huffed while I dug out my handcuffs. He fell in on himself, the fight leaving him as Berke arrived, huffing, to stare down at us. I read him his rights as best I could, given I had done my best impression of a sprinter.

"Jesus, Mary," he panted, hands on his knees, as the crying man I was seated on gave up completely. "You're a speedy fairy."

"It's the wings," I gasped, then moved White Hair to his belly to secure the cuffs.

"What the actual fuck?" Berke asked as I hauled White Hair to his feet. "I mean… Christ, my legs are on fire. What the shit got into you? We're here as backup to SAFE.

This is their bust. You were way out of line on this one, Mary."

I didn't give stepping on toes a second thought when I saw potential—innocent until proven guilty after all—child abusers/traffickers darting out of several doors like rats fleeing a house fire. I simply ran. Instinct. Training. Head up my ass after tongue-fucking a witness in one of my cases. They all were viable excuses, but excuses wouldn't save my ass if our captain got a call from the SAFE captain. Protocol was important. Since I had no good reason for my questionable reaction, I moved on, shoving my suspect ahead of me. Berke came with me, still out of breath, but able to ream me out all the way back to the strip mall where everyone on our side seemed to be in high spirits.

"Body cam was on," I reassured.

The whole chase-and-subdue had *maybe* taken four minutes. In the end, we'd captured ten slimeballs, confiscated thousands of hours of videos about to be shipped off to foreign ports the world over, and took in about forty thousand plus dollars in cash. Thank all the gods for blessed miracles that there were no children on site. The cash we found, I was sure, had been laundered along the way. White Hair proved to be one hell of a songbird, as well as a champion sprinter, because he was singing to all of us like a lark as they were piled into a van to be processed. We had a few names to track down linked to the money laundering, one that we knew rather well and two that were new to us, all thanks to White Hair Sings-A-Lot. With a successful bust under our belts, we all returned to our respective desks after dropping off our gear.

I'd no sooner nodded at Mack, who was coming from court, when the door to my captain's office flew open and my supervisor filled the opening, looking none too happy. Great. Seemed the head of SAFE had made a call.

"How'd court go?" I asked my partner.

Mack grunted while hanging his suit jacket over the back of his squeaky desk chair. There was an odd sort of silence filling our happy little work area.

"Winwood, in my office now," Franks barked. Mack cocked a brow in question. I sighed, shook my head, and walked into Franks' office. The door was open at my back. "Close that door."

Okay, that was never good. I did as I was told, took two steps into the office, and got hit in the face with round after round of irate commander verbal artillery fire. Franks never once sat down. He paced his office, shouting, pointing, and slapping his hands on his desk to make several key points. I nodded. What else could I do? I'd acted irrationally. I should have gotten clearance from my superiors. I should have taken a partner. The list went on and on until Franks, heaving in irritation, stalled out to glare at me.

"Oh, is it my turn to talk?" I asked.

"You talking is a large part of why my ulcers are so bad," he snapped. I opened my mouth to reply. He cut me off with a hand in the air. "No, do not say one word. What I want you to do is tell me why you ran off without a fucking word or a backup. Then, I need you to explain why you fucking tap danced over interdepartmental protocol. Also, and this is maybe the most important, I want you to clarify just what the fuck is wrong with you of late? You were always a wiseass, but the past few months you've been off the rails, Winwood. Do you need some counseling? The department has excellent therapists to help our officers who are struggling with the stress of the job."

"I… no, I don't need therapy." He seemed unconvinced. I was too, if I were being honest. "My caseload is crushing, I'm getting nowhere with the clinic robbery, and my orchid died."

"Orchid your cat or something?"

"No, it's a flower."

"Thank fuck."

"Yeah, I agree." I scrubbed at my face for a moment. "It's a flower. Dead. Been dead for months. I can't seem to throw it away, though. But yeah, sorry, none of that is any excuse for being a dick on a raid. I'll apologize to Captain Klinger over at SAFE."

"You do that, and make sure you grovel nicely. Klinger is a stiff bastard on a good day. As for the workload, I know it's rough. The switch from eight-hour shifts to ten has broiled all of our brains, but the good news is that we have some new blood coming over from various localities. One from Sacramento, and one from La Mesa, so the caseload will lessen in a few weeks."

"That's good. They being paired together?"

"Unlikely." I thought to push to see if these new men would be teamed up with one of our four, but given Franks was apoplectic, I just bobbed my head. "Go make your apologies. And, Winwood, if you are feeling the strain, speak up. We can't afford to lose a good detective over caseload burnout."

I had to wonder how he would feel about the fact I had played tonsil hockey with one of the LA Storm. His blood pressure would rocket. His head would blow off. And his wife would de-nut me with her incredibly long porcelain fingernails.

"I'm good. Just jittery, drank too much last night. I'll call Klinger now and kiss his ass."

"You do that."

Seemed I was dismissed. I slunk out of Franks' office and met the worried glance of my partner and the two elder detectives who had suddenly fallen silent.

"Anyone know the best way to suck a straight guy's dick without actually applying your lips to said dick?" I asked aloud.

The replies I got were varied. None were helpful.

I commenced with the inevitable apologizing aka dick-sucking. Klinger did not give an inch. The call was short, nasty, and filled with simmering ire at my stupidity.

After I hung up, I lifted my thermos to my lips, only to remember that it was empty. Great. No coffee, no smokes, and it was barely noon.

This day could only go upward from here, right?

Chapter Eleven

Oliver

STANDING BY THE ICE, WAITING TO GET OUT FOR WARMUPS for this home game against Carolina, my mind wasn't on the game. Instead, I found myself scanning the stands, searching for a particular face. I had left two tickets at will call for Jackson, seats right on the ice near the goal, and the question whether he'd picked them up gnawed at me. Would he be there? And worse, all I could think was— would he bring a sign?

I had it bad.

We'd texted, had a couple of dates, talked so long into the night I was crabby at early morning practice, and slowly but surely he was stealing tiny bits of my heart.

As my teammates and I started our warmup routine, I subtly maneuvered so I could get a better view of the section I'd left the tickets for. My heart skipped when I spotted him. Jackson was there, and he wasn't alone. Beside him was a young boy, chattering excitedly. Recognition dawned on me; the kid was from one of the youth hockey groups I volunteered with. Michael Zhang's boyfriend, Bryce, was his dad, and yeah, Jackson was his uncle. The kid was fast, loved his hockey, and was always smiling. Jackson, without a sign, was entirely focused on the boy as the kid was explaining something in great detail to his uncle, but his presence in the stands sent a jolt of warmth through me. His lack of a sign didn't matter; his being there was enough.

Ash glided over, following my gaze. "Looking for someone?" he teased, nudging me with his elbow.

"Just seeing if someone took some tickets I left," I replied, trying to sound nonchalant.

Ash followed my gaze and then smirked. "Ah, the cop and his nephew? You left them for the kid?" he asked, even though the smirk was still there.

I couldn't help but smile, feeling Ash's good-natured ribbing. "Not exactly," I said, though I couldn't tear my eyes away from Jackson and Leo.

As warmups continued, I made sure to perform my stretches right in front of where Jackson was seated. It wasn't until I skated close enough to tap the glass with my stick that Jackson looked up, locking eyes with me. He didn't hold a sign, but the wink he sent me spoke louder than any words or playful banners could. It was a silent message, one that echoed in the grin spreading across my face.

Ash caught the exchange and let out a low whistle. "Well, well, if it isn't you making friends with Detective Heartbreaker."

"Just keeping the community engaged," I quipped back, not wanting to delve into the complexities of whatever was developing between Jackson and me.

The whistle blew, signaling the end of warmups. As I skated off the ice, I cast one last glance over my shoulder at Jackson. The excitement on his nephew's face, mirrored by Jackson's own smile, filled me with an unexpected sense of happiness.

He'd come.

During the game, every stride I took on the ice felt amplified, every play charged with an intensity that wasn't solely about the competition. Knowing Jackson was watching from the stands transformed the rink into a stage. I wasn't playing for the win; I was playing for an audience of one, just the same as I used to do with Melissa every time she watched.

That meant something, right?

It wasn't the easiest of games either and, as it progressed, the tension was as thick as the ice beneath our skates. We were tied 2–2, the clock ticking down mercilessly.

Ash, ever the observant partner, shot me a look as we prepared for another face-off. "Time to shine, Cowboy," he muttered, a grin tugging at his lips.

The puck dropped and instinct took over. I found myself in the perfect position as a Carolina player came barreling down with the puck. Without a second thought, I leaned into a hip check; the collision was solid, sending the opposing player sprawling as I scooped up the puck, a rush of adrenaline fueling my movements.

"Beast!" Ash hollered, skating up beside me as we advanced. His praise was a fleeting distraction from the task at hand.

I didn't have a single breath in me to glance towards

the stands, to seek out Jackson's reaction. Instead, I focused on the play, spotting Charles in the perfect position near their goal. With a flick of my wrist, I passed the puck, sending it sliding across the ice, right to Charles' stick.

The moment stretched, the entire arena holding its breath as Charles wound up and took the shot. The puck flew past the goalie, hitting the back of the net with a satisfying *clang*. The arena exploded into a roar of cheers from our fans, the score now 3–2 in our favor.

The bench erupted as we celebrated the go-ahead goal and Ash clapped me on the back, shouting over the noise.

"Told you. Beast mode activated!"

As the final seconds ticked away, and we managed to hold off Carolina's desperate attempts to tie the game, victory was ours. The elation of winning, of overcoming a worthy opponent, was heightened by the knowledge that Jackson had witnessed it all.

When the game ended, and the cheers of the crowd began to fade, I allowed myself a moment to scan the stands. My search found him standing now, clapping, with a smile that reached across the distance between us. There was pride in his eyes, a look that said he understood the language of the game, of my game, more than I'd given him credit for. Maybe it was me hip checking that player, or the way I'd seen the play unfold. I didn't care. I knew he'd seen me, and I was high from thinking about it.

As I skated off the ice with my teammates, celebrating our hard-fought win, I couldn't help but feel that the victory was sweeter than usual. Not only because of the scoreboard, but because of the audience of one who had made the night unforgettable.

In the locker room, amidst the chaos of celebration, Ash nudged me, a knowing glance in his eyes. "You played out of your skin tonight, Ollie. All for the detective?"

I shrugged, a secretive smile playing on my lips. "Maybe," I conceded, my thoughts already drifting to the moment I would see Jackson outside the arena, away from the noise, the ice, and the crowd.

Hopefully soon.

———

I GOT HOME AT ELEVEN. THE HOUSE WAS QUIET EXCEPT FOR the soft hum of the refrigerator and the noise of the television in the back room. Making my rounds first, I visited Daisy's and Scarlett's rooms to kiss them goodnight.

Scarlett stirred as I leaned over, her voice sleepy, but clear. "Did you win, Daddy?"

I smiled, brushing her hair back gently. "Yes, sweetheart, we won."

She smiled, her eyes still closed. "My clever daddy," she murmured before drifting back to sleep.

Feeling a wave of love wash over me, I stared down at her for the longest time, lost in memories of the day I'd first held her, letting the grief in when I remembered Melissa, and then, somehow feeling better that I could handle the grief.

Would you like him? I asked her as I headed downstairs

and stopped at a photo of us on our wedding day. We'd been so young, only seventeen, but she'd been the center of my world. Still was, actually, given the two girls she'd gifted me. I kissed the tips of my fingers and pressed them to the photo. "I don't know what I'm doing, Mel. I miss you."

I carried on to the living room where Jamie was sprawled on the couch, watching an episode of *Who Wants to Be a Millionaire*? He barely glanced up as I joined him.

"Good game?" he asked. He wasn't a hockey fan at all, citing the fact that being a Brit meant it was his God-given duty to be a football fan, and not the one with the "*funny-shaped balls*"—his words not mine—but real football with his favorite team, Liverpool.

"We won."

He made a roaring crowd noise. "Go, Storm!"

I smacked him upside the head and let the soft sofa swallow me. On screen, Jimmy Kimmel was asking which out of four U.S. Presidents appeared on Mount Rushmore. The contestant seemed confused, and Jamie threw a cushion at the screen.

"Oh my god, I'm not even American, and I know it's Lincoln! Fuck me, this is only the one thousand question, and that's dollars, not even *real* money!" He deadpanned the last of it, and it was my turn to throw a cushion at him.

Finally, the poor contestant, Jimmy from Maine, gave the correct answer, but not until he'd gone through his reasoning, which frustrated Jamie even more.

I was too distracted by my phone, eagerly hoping I'd get a message from Jackson, and giving him another ten minutes before I texted first.

I didn't have to because, soon enough, my phone buzzed with a new message.

> Jackson: You were on fire tonight.

He added a fire emoji and a hockey stick.

I couldn't help the grin that spread across my face as I typed back.

> Oliver: Only because I knew you were watching

Was it wrong adding a winky flirty face? If it was, then whatever, because I sent five of them.

The exchange went on, each message flirtier than the last.

> Jackson: Do you always do that sexy stretching thing before the game?

> Oliver: Yep

> Jackson: I think you should stop in case half the arena combusts at the sight of your ass.

Oh my god. *Oh my god*.

> Oliver: I'll stop then. But when the Storm loses all their games, it's on you.

> Jackson: Hmmmm. Maybe I should just come to every game. Just in case.

> Oliver: Guess I'll have to make sure you get season tickets then. Only fair.

> Jackson: Only if you promise to score a
> goal for me next time.

> Oliver: It's a deal. I'll score for you
> any day.

Jamie, eventually noticing the smile I couldn't wipe off my face, paused the show. "Okay, out with it. Who's put that grin on your face? Is it your sexy detective?"

I hesitated, the warmth from Jackson's messages still lingering. "Maybe."

Jamie raised an eyebrow but didn't press.

> Jackson: I can't stop thinking about
> that kiss

> Oliver: Me neither

> Oliver: I want to do it again

Shit. I was straight-up, blushing now, the heat prickling my skin.

> Jackson: I want to kiss you some more

> Jackson: Everywhere

> Oliver: Me too.

> Jackson: Jesus, I have to go to bed. I'm
> up at five

> Oliver: Thinking of me?

> Jackson: I am now. Night. Xx

> Oliver: Night xx

My inner teenager was amped for the kisses, and the fact Jackson was thinking of me. Gah. I needed to get my tired self to bed and think about the kiss.

Or more like get myself off thinking about him kissing me all over.

And hope to hell, one day, it wouldn't just be my imagination.

Soon.

Chapter Twelve

Jackson

"So, then she made this dessert that was low calorie and had pineapple in it," Mack said as we left the courthouse for our lunch break. We'd been giving our account of what had happened about seven months ago during a sting operation. We'd run to shut down some massage parlors that were selling more than hot rocks and foot rubs. Body parts had been getting rubbed, but they weren't toes.

I nodded as we walked, the day a cloudy one, big rains moving in with high winds. The rain was sorely needed. No one wanted wildfires. Of course, with the storms came the possibility of lightning, which could spark the one thing we all wished to avoid. Sort of like me texting Oliver all the time.

We were not talking about the case either. We were flirting. Bigly. Even though I knew it was wrong, I could not stop myself from replying with my own idiotic brand of come hither that worked on no man other than Oliver. He seemed to dig my snark, go figure. This little message was about a local politician who had been caught with his hand in the cookie jar over in the San Fran area. Lots of romance with a fellow office worker, funds being spent on jewelry to woo said fellow office worker. Big, expensive cookies.

"What do you think?"

I glanced up from telling Oliver that I hoped he didn't expect me to spend ten grand on a dinner date because I'd have to sell my car and then, how would I get to the luxury restaurant to woo him. Woo him. I had actually typed those words. On my phone. To Oliver. Honestly, I was beyond help.

The Santa Ana winds threw my tie into my face. I batted it down, then stared at my partner. Mack huffed before shoving past me to get in line at a small taco shack.

"Sorry, I was discussing the merits of quality linens with my sister."

Mack shot me a glare over his shoulder as we waited to get into the tiny eatery. "Talking to your sister makes you smile like your head is empty? And it is, you know. Empty."

"It's not totally empty. There's enough gray matter to tell you that you should stay far away from anything on the menu that has beans in it. The last time you overdid it on the refried beans and had to go back to court to continue your testimony, the judge had to empty the courtroom to bring in fumigators."

"Fuck you. They only cleared the courtroom for a few minutes while the bailiff used some Febreze. And don't change the subject. I know you're not talking to Courtney, Bryce, or Leo. You're talking to Cowan, and that is going to bite you on the ass." The mere thought of Oliver nipping my bare ass made my dick twitch. "There. See, that expression right there is what I'm talking about! Fuck me, Jackson, you are walking a really fine line. You know that having a sexual relationship with that man is going to potentially screw the pooch on that investigation. All the defense would have to do is get wind of you being involved with a witness during an active investigation, and you'd be on the stand faster than you can spit."

"I'm not involved with Oliver. We're just…" I floundered.

Mack leapt on that mumble with both feet. "Yeah, exactly. Do you not recall what we were warned about when we were in training?" I rolled my eyes. "Don't do that. They said that the three things that will bring down a male officer the fastest is booze, bucks, and broads. Those are the three B's to avoid, Jackson."

"For me, it would be booze, bucks, and beef bayonet." Mack did not look amused. "Okay, look, I know you're just trying to do good by me. I know that, and I appreciate it. There is nothing sexual between me and Oliver." He snorted in derision. "I mean it. Look, to prove that I'm not smitten, I am going to go to his house tonight and explain that, while I enjoy his texts, I have to maintain my professionalism."

"Yeah?" He took a step closer to the door of the taco shack. The sidewalk was bustling with people trying to eat and get back to work.

I made an *X* over my heart. "I promise. I'm going to fill him in on the latest news of the case, which is fucking little, and then tell him that, until the case is solved or closed, we're to only have contact when it has to do with the investigation."

"You could tell him now," he suggested, then glanced at the phone in my hand. Yeah, I could. I should. I knew this flirty/kissy thing we had bubbling was not cool. Mack was right. If the case did ever get to court and the defense attorney found out there was something sexual between one of the detectives and a key witness, it could be ugly. *Real* ugly. Any testimony that I or Oliver had given would be tainted. I'd probably be brought up on charges of conduct unbecoming. Possibly fired. So, ending it now, before it had a chance of really getting out of control, was the right thing to do. And I would. Tonight.

"I'm not the kind of man to do something like this over a text."

Mack studied me for a long moment, then sighed. "Okay, tell him in person. Tomorrow, I want to hear that you're done staring at your phone like a teenager who's been shown his first pair of titties." His cell vibrated, and he checked it. "Financial reports are in from the clinic and staff," he advised.

"Great, hours of sitting and looking at numbers," I growled.

"Not you. It'll be me, now you're fucking one of the witnesses. So, I'll take over any witness contacts with Oliver Cowan starting on the morrow."

I blinked. "'On the morrow'? What the fuck? Am I partnered with Billy Shakespeare?" I reached into my front pocket for my smokes, only to realize I didn't have any. Oh hey, that was progress. I'd not thought about a cigarette for almost ten minutes. Fuck you, nicotine addiction. God,

I was more than hungry now. This line was stupid long. If I flashed my badge, would it get us served faster? Probably not…

"Elena and I have been watching *Bridgerton*," Mack said, his pale cheeks turning red.

That busted me up. Mack chuckled. I didn't mention that I had been known to watch that show on occasion. Occasion meaning as soon as the episodes dropped. I wasn't one to miss hot men in tight breeches when the opportunity presented itself. Speaking of hot men, I snuck in one final text to Oliver saying I had to go and would drop by this evening if that suited. It did suit, he replied, then signed off with several cookie emojis. I smiled at the chocolate chips until someone—Mack—elbowed me in the ribs. Hard. Right. No more of that stuff. It was time to return to being the old Jackson Winwood, even if I wasn't sure I truly wanted to go back.

I COULD HEAR THE FRIVOLITY INSIDE OLIVER'S HOUSE from on the front step. I listened for a minute or two, enjoying the sound of giggling girls, stampeding feet, and the burly growl of a man pretending to be a troll… maybe?

The squeals reminded me of my youth when my older sister and I played outside. Our folks didn't like screaming in the house. Dad was especially touchy about loud kids, and so our rowdiness always took place in the backyard. Generally, I would be told to be something gross and nasty, say a troll, and Courtney would be the fair princess who would slay me. None of that waiting for a prince to rescue her for my big sis. Nope. She took care of her own business, and if killing the tiny troll who had stolen her stuffed piggy was what needed to be done, then so be it.

I missed my sister. And my nephew. I wished we lived closer to each other, but that wasn't going to happen. Maybe if Court were living in LA still, I'd be more… I don't know. Social? Pleasant? Less prone to being sullen and sad all the fucking time. It struck me, then, standing on Oliver's stoop, that one of the things I liked about him, and his house, was that when I was here I wasn't alone. I had no one, really. Mack and I were close, but I didn't go to his place even though I was invited every week. He and Elena were newlyweds. They didn't really want some half-drunk asshole sitting around making their lives sour and stale.

Someone peeked out of the window beside the door, yanking the sheer curtain to the side, her tiny face pressed to the glass. I snickered at the little girl, doing her best impression of a pug dog. Then, without warning, the door opened. There stood two girls with long hair, bright eyes, and glittery wings.

"Hello, sir," the oldest of the two, Scarlett, said. She of the clever blue eyes and long dark hair like Oliver. Daisy, the younger, stood at her sister's side, both winded and sweaty.

"Hello, is your father home?" I asked in my nicest cop voice just as Oliver dashed into view, his eyes widening as he spied me in the doorway. He was wearing a dragon headpiece and a lumpy tail someone had tied to his belt.

"Ah, I see that a fearsome dragon has eaten your dad. I'm the Sheriff! How can I save you?"

Oliver rolled his eyes as he struggled to free himself

from the felt dragon head sitting on his skull, but he was smiling. The girls giggled in delight.

"Help us, Sheriff! We have to get the dragon!" Scarlett shouted, turned, and ran at her father. Daisy did the same.

Oliver gathered them both up, growling and snarling most fearsomely. His dark eyes moved to me. "Take another step, Sheriff, and I will eat the princesses," he snarled in very good dragon speak.

I leaped into the foyer. The girls squealed in glee. Oliver flashed me a smile that made my knees turn into jelly, and the chase was on. This one was much more enjoyable than the last chase I'd been involved in. This one ended when we all collapsed onto a massive sofa in the living room, out of breath, but laughing madly.

"Okay, the sheriff… needs to buy a horse," I huffed as the girls jumped up, giddy with energy, and ran off to find me a horse. Oliver glanced at me, a quick peek that could have been purposely seductive, and my whole body rang like a tuning fork.

"Thank you for playing along," he said, his breathing calming much faster than mine. Damn athletes who never smoked.

I waved his thanks off. It had been incredibly fun for me to take part in some playtime. Leo and I never got enough time together, it seemed, what with his father wanting him all to himself, which I got, but still…

"The law does what the law needs to do," I replied, noting with interest that his gaze was moving over me as I lay sprawled on his couch.

Knowing he was checking me out, I did the opposite of what I should have done. I should have sat up, told him why I was here, and left, pronto. Instead, I flexed my hips just a bit to show off the growing bulge in my slacks. Oliver's gaze grew hot.

The girls came thundering in then, both with stick horses in hand. I shoved a throw pillow in front of my groin, then begged off a gallop, citing my old age. The girls moaned but moved on to their own games.

"Is there something new about the case?" Oliver asked.

"No, sadly, nothing really, but we're not giving up," I assured him. He seemed placated with my reply. Now was the time to lay my upstanding cop dictate on him, only there was someone missing. "Where's your friend, the nanny?"

"Jamie?"

Of course, I knew his name, but my inner child poked at me. "Yeah, Jamie."

"At a research conference, he's away for the night."

Well, that was interesting news. Not that there weren't the girls to think of, but we might be able to get in a peck or two when the girls weren't watching. I'd take that.

I was starved for a taste of Oliver.

I came here to stop everything, not start something.

"Dinner will be ready in a few minutes, if you'd like to stay?" Oliver enquired as he peeled off his dragon tail and placed it on the coffee table next to a coloring book and box of crayons.

Nope, negatory. Tell him what you came here for and leave.

"What are you having?" I asked as Inner Jackson gave me a hearty Moe Howard slap to the head.

"Spaghetti and meatballs. Nothing fancy. Oh, and a salad that only I will eat."

God, that sounded amazing. "I'd like that."

"Good. Want to help set the table?"

I stuffed lonely old Jackson into the trunk of a mental Ford Pinto. Who needed his negativity? I'd tell Oliver why I was here after we ate. Might as well get a meal in me before I went back to talking to a dead orchid while sipping whiskey and wishing I had someone to hold on to when shit went south.

I WANTED HIM.

When we were washing dishes. Or when he was upstairs tucking the girls into bed. Even if his house smelled of garlic, baby shampoo, and a Barbie that had been soaked in perfume and left to dry on the kitchen counter.

I wanted Oliver. Badly. And that was a recipe for disaster. Yet here I stood, sipping coffee in his subtly lit, homey kitchen, examining the artwork on the fridge. Deep down, I knew I was about to screw the pooch, but I was caught in a riptide that I couldn't free myself from.

I suspected Oliver was in the same predicament. Only his career didn't hinge on us sleeping together. He would be fine. Me, on the other hand…

I felt him enter the room, that was how strong his pull was. My eyes closed as I willed myself to dredge up the courage to turn and tell him how things were going to be.

"They're out cold," he informed me softly, his voice like warm honeyed tea soothing a sore throat.

I opened my eyes, then turned to face him. Something taut snapped to life between us. I could no more stop myself from moving toward him than I could stop the world from spinning. Hopelessly adrift, I placed my mug of coffee on the counter, his deep brown gaze on me as I walked to him and sifted my fingers through his hair.

"This is going to be incredible," I whispered to the small part of Jackson not being controlled by my cock.

"We have to be quiet," he replied with a raspy exhale that stripped away any worries as I pulled his lips to mine. Covering his mouth would keep him silent. We went at each other like starving jackals. Nipping, lapping, biting. My dick was throbbing in my shorts, leaking, wanting…

"I want you in my mouth," I growled as I nibbled a path from his puffy lips to his neck. I bit gently, but firmly. Marking him. He moaned low and long, his hands moving down my sides to lock me into place against his body. I sucked harder. He rolled his hips. My balls drew up instantly, so I broke free. "I'm close."

With that announcement, I went to my knees. Oliver took a step back to bolster himself against the fridge as I yanked his joggers and briefs to his ankles. A fat, long prick sprang up and nearly put my eye out. If I was going to be blinded, let it be by a dick. I took him in hand, drool filling my mouth, and gave the purple head a swipe. Salty pre-cum coated my tongue. A soft sound of pleasure escaped me before I took him to the root.

"Fuck," he growled, his hips jutting. I gagged. He tried to pull back, but I grabbed his ass to keep him in place. I could take it. Fuck my mouth anytime, hockey man. "Sorry… it's been so long and you… ah man, that is good."

I purred around his dick, pulling a sound from him that made me shudder. Never had I heard such a perfect noise from a lover. I began sucking frantically, frenzied almost to get his spunk down my throat. He tried, bless him. He really did try not to blow his nut too quickly, but when I took his hefty balls in my hand and tugged them, he pumped like a mad man, then came down my throat. My eyes rolled back in my head as the tang of him coated my tongue.

I wanted more. I sucked with more vigor, slurping, drooling, moaning around his pulsating cock until he carded his fingers into my hair and eased me off. I glanced up and got the most blissful smile I had ever seen.

"You are… that was…"

"Incredible," I supplied, then swiped my lips with my tongue. Oliver shuddered at the sight, then gave my hair a tug. I rose slowly, then moved into his arms. He kissed me deeply, his tongue rolling over my molars as he unzipped my jeans to free my aching prick. Once he had me in his strong, rough hands, I went to pieces quickly. His head back, his mouth on my jugular, he stroked me tip to root, his calloused palm twirling over my sensitive cockhead. "Oh, damn, yeah…"

That was the extent of my monologue. He gave my throat a lick, then lowered himself to the floor. I watched as he dipped the tip of his tongue into the slit. That was pretty much all she wrote. I grunted out something that might have been a warning. Could have been the seven-day forecast. Who knew? My brain had shut down the moment I'd said hello this evening. I came hard, my head snapping back so fiercely my neck cracked. My balls emptied themselves into his willing mouth. I pumped gently until he pulled off, his lips coated with spittle and spunk.

"Jesus Christ, that was…"

"Incredible?" he offered, and I could do nothing other than nod. When he was standing, we kissed, exploring each other's mouths at leisure now that the madness of blind lust had been sated. For now. When I looked into his warm, open eyes, I knew this was the beginning of something more powerful and compelling than anything I had ever experienced. I should leave now. Right now. This instant. It had only been oral sex, not intercourse. I was sure my superiors would see the difference. Hell, that reasoning had worked for a president…

"I usually don't let myself get that carried away in the kitchen. Or anywhere where the girls could walk in," he said. I nodded. "You're just so…"

"Yeah, you are too."

"I can warm up some coffee cake that Jamie baked yesterday. If you'd like to stay and talk or…" He shrugged, and I smiled, as we both tucked and zipped.

Yeah, I felt the same way. "I'd like some coffee cake and talk."

His eyes danced with happiness, and I knew I was a goner.

Chapter Thirteen

Oliver

THE WARMTH FROM THE KITCHEN STILL LINGERED AS WE sat down, the air between us charged with something very new. The cake, fresh from the oven, steamed slightly when I cut into it, its sweet aroma filling the space. I served us both generous slices, accompanied by heavy cream and the rich, comforting smell of freshly brewed coffee.

Melissa would have loved that I was finally acting on what she'd asked me to do, I thought, a pang of sorrow threading through the sweetness of the moment. I glanced at Jackson, who seemed to sense the shift in my mood.

"You okay?" he asked, his voice gentle, eyes full of concern.

I nodded, taking a moment to gather my thoughts. "I was just thinking about my wife, Melissa," I admitted, the words feeling both heavy and freeing. "She had a way of making even the simplest moments feel special, and she always wanted me to shake free from the cancer and her leaving."

Jackson reached across the table, his hand brushing mine in a gesture of comfort. "She sounds special," he said.

"She was," I replied, a tiny smile finding its way through the sadness.

"Can you tell me about her?" Jackson's voice was soft, treading lightly on a topic that still felt raw to me. "I'd like to know."

I took a deep breath, the memories flooding back with a clarity that pained me. "We met when I was still at school, childhood sweethearts and all that. She hated hockey; I played hockey. She was clever; me, not so much, so she helped me on a project for Chemistry. Next thing I know, we were engaged and married. I loved her from the first moment I saw her." I huffed a laugh. It really had been love at first sight. "Then, we had the girls, but after Melissa... after she found the lump..." I pressed a hand to my chest. "It was like being hit by a truck. We were in the doctor's office, and they told us... they told us she had six months, maybe a year, with treatment." The words felt heavy on my tongue, each one a reminder of the helplessness I'd felt. "She decided against the treatment, wanted her time with the girls to be at home."

"I can't even imagine how you both felt."

"Lost. Strong. I don't know."

"How did *you* manage? With the kids being so young?" Jackson's question was gentle.

I chuckled mirthlessly. "'Manage'? I don't know if I did, really. The four of us focused on making memories, on giving Daisy and Scarlett as much time with their mom as we could. Then, when it got close, we contacted an agency, and Jamie came to the house to help with the girls, temporary at first, and Melissa and me…" Emotion caught in my chest. "She was incredible, right to the end."

"And Jamie stayed?"

"He did. He was with us until we left New York, but he's back now, to stay for good, or so he says."

Jackson nodded; his expression was somber. "And after? How did you…?"

I looked away, finding a spot on the wall to focus on, anything to keep the emotions at bay. "After is a blur. I threw myself into being a dad. It was the only thing that made sense. Grief… it changes you. It's there, always, but you learn to live with it, to build around it."

The room was silent for a moment, the weight of the conversation settling over us like a blanket.

Jackson finally broke the silence. "Oliver, I can't even begin to imagine what you went through. But I want you to know I'm here. For whatever you need. If you just need a friend in a new city, or you want… something else. I'm here."

"Thank you, Jackson," I said, meeting his gaze. "That means a lot."

"I'm sorry for your loss," he said, and it wasn't handed out by rote—he actually meant he was sorry, and sadness flooded his expression.

"She left me with the two most wonderful parts of her —Daisy and Scarlett."

"She did," he said and smiled.

I loved his smile. I didn't want to see him sad.

He continued, "But sometimes, I worry… Am I

enough for them? Am I doing this— being a dad— right? And then, I get traded and take the girls from everything they know, then I meet you, and I don't know anything anymore. Everything is upside down."

J ACKSON SQUEEZED MY HAND, HIS GAZE STEADY. "F ROM what I've seen, you're more than enough. I'm not the best at knowing this, but they love you, so I'd say you're a good dad."

His words made me smile, and our fingers stayed laced on the table.

"I still wear my wedding ring." I glanced at him, trying to gauge his reaction.

He shrugged, as if that didn't faze him at all. "It's her connection to you, to the girls. Why would you take it off?"

Oh fuck, he just said the absolutely perfect thing, and I had to change the subject before I completely lost control and demanded he take me upstairs right then.

I made sure our conversation drifted to lighter topics, laughter mingling with the clink of forks on plates. But as the last bites of cake disappeared, Jackson grew quiet, his expression turning serious.

"There was a reason I came here tonight, something I need to tell you," he began, his hand tightening around mine. "Because you're a key witness in the case… I shouldn't even be here. If we… if this," he gestured between us, "is going to be anything, I have to recuse myself."

The weight of his words settled on us, heavy and real.

My heart raced, caught between the fear of what losing him could mean and the depth of what I was beginning to feel.

"I want more with you. Not just the kisses, but the cake and the coffee and the stupid messaging." Jackson said, his voice a whisper of certainty. "Do you want more with me? Because if you do, I'm walking into the station tomorrow and taking myself off the case."

The question hung in the air, fraught with implications and possibilities. I looked at him, *really* looked, seeing not simply the detective or the casual acquaintance from the rink, but the man who'd walked into my kitchen and somehow, unexpectedly, into my heart.

"Yes," I said, the word a testament to everything I felt, everything I hoped for. "I want more with you."

Jackson's smile was like a promise, one I felt down to my bones. We kissed briefly, and it was enough to seal the deal.

He didn't stay—I was alone with my girls, and I needed space.

I think he needed space.

Only, he had a hard time leaving—or I had a hard time letting him go. I found myself pinned against the cool wall, the texture of the paint barely registering against my back as Jackson's body pressed close to mine. His hands were firm on my waist, drawing me in, eliminating any space that remained between us. The urgency of this goodbye kiss caught me off guard and it was as if the world outside this bubble we'd created had ceased to exist.

Jackson's mouth moved against mine and the kiss

deepened, but slowed, and I found myself responding with equal passion, my hands tangling in his hair, pulling him closer, as if I could somehow merge us into one. His scent enveloped me, a mix of the crispness from the outside air and something uniquely him, intoxicating and grounding all at once.

Time seemed to warp, moments stretching out as I sunk into the kisses.

We finally parted, foreheads resting together as we caught our breath. His beautiful green eyes, when they met mine, were a storm of emotions, and he pressed himself against me, our cocks hard.

"What you do to me," he whispered, then brushed his thumb across my cheek. "Oliver," he whispered, my name on his lips sounding like a vow. He moved a little. I leaned back, and all too soon, we were kissing and grinding slow and steady against each other. I laced my hands behind his neck and held him there, the kisses becoming nothing more than exchanging tender words in the darkness of the hallway.

"Fuck," I muttered, closing my eyes, so close *just* from this.

"Open your eyes, Oliver," he ordered in the softest tone, and I opened them as he captured one last kiss. And then, we were coming where we stood, arching into each other, losing our heads completely.

We stood for a while, wrapped in each other's arms, but then it was time for him to leave, and I had to let him go.

"Eww," I joked.

He pressed a kiss to the tip of my nose. "At least you don't have to drive home in it," he deadpanned.

One more kiss.

Then another.

And finally, he left.

Chapter Fourteen

Jackson

THAT NIGHT, FOR THE FIRST TIME IN WEEKS—HELL, MAYBE months—I was out as soon as my head hit the pillow. No weird dreams from the nicotine patches, no rolling around like a rotisserie chicken while slapping the shit out of my pillow, no getting up to sit on my bare patio with a dead plant and a bottle of Wild Turkey. I slept like a baby.

For three hours.

The buzzing of an incoming call crept into my rest bit by bit. I came to consciousness slowly, moaning as I woke, my face buried in the pillow.

"Why, Lord?" I mumbled as I peeled one eye open to find my alarm clock. Ten minutes after three. "Are you fucking kidding me?"

I rolled from the bed, eyes bleary, nothing to cover my naked ass, and began the search for my phone. I found it in the bathroom in the medicine cabinet. Why there? Not a fucking clue. I grabbed it, slammed the cabinet door shut, then grimaced at my reflection. Shit, I looked like hell warmed over and topped with crap. A crap pancake. What the hell did Oliver see in this exhausted mug?

The phone continued buzzing like a demented bee. I tapped the green button and placed it to my ear. My hair was a mess, my face pale, and my eyes were like two piss holes in the snow.

"Unless someone is dead…" I growled to my partner.

"As a matter of fact," Mack replied around a yawn. Some of the lethargy left me. A tiny bit. "Some coked-up stripper just found our clinic gunman stuffed behind a dumpster behind the Pickle Palace."

"Did you say Pickle Palace?"

"What? No, what? Pickle Palace? Were you out drinking tonight? I said Purple Palace. It's that ratty strip club over on—"

"I know where it is. And no, I wasn't drinking."

I was sucking the dick of a key witness, buddy. Bet that beats a few shots at the local bar in terms of worrisome behavior.

"Good. Elena and I worry about you. Meet me at the Palace in ten. Beat cops are locking down the scene, but homicide has already been called. If we want any chance to even get a peep at the body—"

"Yep, I'll be there in ten. Eight, if I can skip putting on underwear."

"You do you." Mack hung up.

I splashed water on my face, rushed to dress, and jumped into my car. The ride took exactly six minutes if one raced through a few yellow lights.

Several girls in skimpy attire stood around the rear of the seedy establishment known as the Purple Palace. I parked next to a brick wall the color of a plum, grabbed a stick of gum, and walked over to where a couple of uniformed cops were talking to a woman in a thong and sparkly fishnet stockings. Her upper half was covered with a towel she clasped to her breasts. Tears flowed down her face.

Mack stood over the body, his hair as mussed as mine, chewing on a pen cap.

"Imagine meeting you here," I quipped as I strolled up, showing my badge to one of the patrolmen as I ducked under some flapping yellow crime scene tape.

"We have to stop meeting like this. My wife is going to get jealous," Mack replied, yawned, then pointed at the body with a pen. "Meet one Periapsis Lane."

I took a knee beside the dead man, careful not to kneel in the ever-widening puddle of blood and brain matter. "The witness who called it in, Helga Smithers, over there," he jerked a thumb at the dancer with the fishnets sobbing on a cop's shoulder. "Said she stepped outside to have a smoke and found him hiding in the space between the wall and the dumpster. Thinking the man was sleeping one off, she gave him a shout and a push. That's when he toppled over, showing Ms. Smithers that one side of his head was missing. She screamed, ran inside, and then someone in the club called the cops. Midge over there gave me a heads up when they arrived because of the small tattoo on the back of his hand that matched the one on our suspect."

My focus left Mack's tired face to focus on the back of Mr. Lane's left hand. Yep, same stupid smiley face. "She and her partner made jokes about it when the initial APB went out a few weeks ago. And before you asked, yes,

Midge and I dated for about two weeks when I first joined the force. Elena knows. You can stop thinking dirty things."

"As if I ever think dirty things," I replied as I rose, taking careful steps around the corpse. "Looks fresh. Blood is barely congealed, and it's warm tonight. I gather no one inside heard the gunshots?"

"Doubtful, what with the music. Midge and her partner are ready to sign off on the scene now that we're here."

"Okay, yeah, we'll start talking to the witnesses before homicide shows up waving their dicks around."

Mack muttered something, then walked off to get as much information as we could. I eyeballed the guy on the ground for a moment longer as his unusual name tickled something in the far corner of my sleep-deprived and suddenly smitten mind. When it hit me, I pulled out a pair of latex gloves from my back pocket and eased Peri's wallet from his back pocket. Nothing much in it. A few stolen debit cards—his name was not on the cards—a small cube of hash wrapped in foil, a condom, a few twenties, and a California driver's license. Bingo. I took a picture of the license, shoved everything back into the wallet, and placed it on his chest. Then, I noticed the corner of a photo and tugged it free. This was the original photo from the clinic, and I held it up to the light, then bagged it.

"So, he did take it then," Mack commented.

"Seems he did." I passed the bag up to Mack and something caught my eye, and I pointed at it. "Writing on the back."

He turned it over, and we stared at random words and letters on a list.

"Jesus Christ, tell me this isn't some coded shit that leads to buried treasure," Mack snarled.

I snapped a photo of the back and pocketed my cell. Then, I peeled off my gloves and turned to Mack, who had been pulled away by an older man who, it seemed, ran the club given that his T-shirt read *MANAGER* on the back. And my first boyfriend had said that all those years of studying Criminal Justice at UC Irvine were a waste of time. Fuck you, Adam. I'm now a detective making tons of... well, okay, maybe not tons, but... fuck Adam anyway, just because.

"Mack, let's see if we can wake up a judge to get a warrant for Peri's home address."

"But the witnesses," Mack began, and I waved it off.

Homicide was en route, along with the coroner. Both of them would rip me a new one for messing around with the body, so us leaving to do something else seemed a good idea. I'd fill in the showboats in homicide later because I was a good Joe who always played nice with other people's toys. If we could tie the dead man to Ivan Baladin, which I assumed we could, since the moron had shouted Baladin's name after hitting Joe the Good Doctor, we could pull Baladin in for questioning. It might be flimsy at best, but if the judge went along with it, we'd be able to haul Ivan in for a chat. I liked to chat with criminals at the crack of dawn. It always got me hard. And it would postpone my talk with Franks, so a win/win.

IVAN BALADIN WAS NOT A HAPPY CAMPER. MACK AND I were seated in a viewing room with another cop, Dennis, watching the man slowly simmer—like a pot of marinara, but far less appealing. The micro-camera in the corner was damn good. Showed us the little droplets of sweat on his brow and picked up all the mutterings he was making. Nothing of use, sadly, but he was agitated, that was for sure.

"How long has he been in there now?" Mack asked. I poured some fresh coffee from my Minnie thermos into my Minnie pink cup, sipped, sighed, then grinned at my partner.

"About an hour."

I opened the file one more time, checking through the information we'd pulled from evidence at our dead attacker's shitty apartment. Two names had been prominent—Ivan Baladin, wannabee gangster, evil asshole, and all around fucked-up fucker, and much to our surprise, the name of the sweetly innocent, always crying, Heloise Grant.

Turned out, Heloise was as deep into Ivan's money laundering shit as she could be, which was why we had her cooling off in the next room over.

"Always the crying ones," I muttered as we stared in at her.

She wasn't crying now. We'd left her sitting there, back straight, staring at the door with a dead expression. Gone was the simpering and the crying and the innocent act. Instead, she'd demanded a lawyer and clammed up.

Her financial records were on their way, and not the surface stuff we'd already requested, but a deep dive into where the hell she was keeping the money she'd skimmed from the clinic. Turned out, she'd been laundering money as donations through Haven of Hope, and Ivan was about to go down.

He just didn't know it yet.

"Think we should go in and harass Ivan now?" I asked.

Mack scratched the red whiskers on his chin and nodded. So, we eased out of our chairs, gave Dennis a pat on the shoulder, and made our way to interrogation room 4. Dennis would be watching and recording what went on throughout the conversation, as he would be with several other interrogations. Technology had made the old one-way mirror a thing of the past.

We sauntered in as if we had no cares in the world. Ivan's shark-like eyes darted from his hands resting on the cold steel table to us.

"I want a lawyer," he said immediately.

"You're not under arrest, Ivan," I pointed out while lowering my tired-as-fuck ass into a chair across from him. "We brought you in for some routine questioning in relation to the murder of one of your employees. A Periapsis Lane."

"Never heard of him. I want my lawyer," Ivan barked, his upper lip damp with perspiration.

"Sure, sure, of course you do, and she's on the way. Lawyers hate early wake-ups," Mack said as he shoved a cup of black coffee across the table to Ivan with his most engaging smile. Ivan wasn't buying our nice cop routine. He was smarter than the average bear, or the average hood, who got easily identifiable tattoos, then attacked innocent people. "Have some coffee. It's not great, but it's free."

Ivan glowered at my partner, then turned his sights to me. "You're violating my rights."

"Are we? I don't see how. When we arrived at your home at five-fifteen a.m., your wife let us in of her own free will. You agreed to come down and shoot the shit. So now, here we are, having a little talk."

"I got nothing to say to either of you until my lawyer arrives."

"Aw, that's too bad. We have so many things to talk with you about, Ivan. I enjoy chit-chatting and discussions with upstanding citizens such as yourself. Sometimes, I learn new words and phrases when I spend time bullshitting with others. Just the other day, I discovered that the Korean word for horse is mal, but it's pronounced my, or that was how it sounded to me."

Ivan's eyebrows knitted. "You hauled me from bed to talk Korean?"

"No, we're talking about new words and phrases. I have one for you." I leaned over the table just a little. "Do you know what the term probable cause means?"

His thin lips pressed tightly together.

"No idea? Well, it means that the police, that's us, can bring in people whom we strongly suspect have been involved in a crime. Sometimes, like this morning, the police get a warrant to enter the home of a low-level guy who beat up a veteran in a medical center. Then they find all kinds of incriminating stuff that some poor slob left lying around his place. Stuff like journals with the names of people they work for and what kind of jobs they were hired to do because that person liked to think of themselves as a writer. Can you imagine anyone being so stupid as to work for a criminal sort, then jotting down his daily activities? Me either, and yet here we are, me, you, and Mack here, sitting on four notebooks full of that incriminating evidence that has your name in just about every entry. Ain't life funny that way, Ivan? So, want to tell us why you hired an attacker to go after Joseph Quinan?"

Ivan grew eerily quiet. I saw that brief glimmer of worry in his feral gaze.

"Did you know that we found all kinds of evidence of… well, hell, what is that phrase, Mack?"

"Money laundering?" Mack supplied, then took a sip of coffee.

I snapped my fingers. "That's it. Money laundering. Your boy Periapsis was a religious note taker. You'd think that he might have been trying to protect himself in case something untoward happened to him. Anyway, those notes tell a really interesting story about medical fraud, Ivan. Yep, I know, I was shocked as well. Seems your name came up a lot, as well as the name of one Heloise Grant, who takes care of the books at the Haven of Hope clinic. We haven't had time to sort through it all yet. Oh we will, rest assured, but there're all kinds of hinky stuff going on. Phantom billings, over billings, and even a shell company owned by your wife in which you seem to be the sole member of the governing board. How on earth did that happen, do you think?"

Ivan began to sweat in earnest. Yeah, morning chats with felons were great fun. Not. Neither was watching some scumbag walk away after paying tons of cash for bail, but that was part of the legal system. Even dirtbags deserved a day in court to be judged by their peers.

CHATS WITH YOUR PARTNER LATER IN THE DAY, HOWEVER, weren't half as much fun.

"Okay, so here's the thing," I opened with. "My relationship with Oliver crossed a line last night that I cannot step back from any longer, nor do I want to."

Mack looked gutted. "Was that what the big talk with Franks was earlier?"

I nodded. "I told him that I was developing feelings for Oliver Cowan, and he for me, and asked to be removed from the case. I assume either you'll get the nod, or the dynamic Boomer duo will. That's Franks' call, obviously."

"I told you not to get involved with him," he moaned as we sat outside the precinct on a stone bench donated by the family of an LAPD officer killed in the line of duty fifteen years ago. The sun was bright, the winds warm, and my mood bittersweet.

"The heart wants what the heart wants," I said with a sluggish lift of a shoulder. "I don't think I've ever felt this way about anyone before. It scares the living shit out of me, Mack."

He sighed, then nudged me in the side with a bony elbow. "Now you know how I feel about Elena."

"Yeah, I guess I do." I'd teased him pretty hard the first two years they'd dated. When things had gotten serious, and he'd proposed, I'd been even more of a sarcastic twit. "I don't know what he sees in me, to be honest. I'm a rundown cop. He's a fucking superstar athlete. He has kids, and a house, and green plants on stands in the windows. I got nothing like that, and yet, when he kisses me…"

"Okay, yeah, I don't need all the gory details of gay butt stuff." He stood and looked down at me, his freckled cheeks rounding into a warm smile. "I'm glad you found someone. Fuck knows you needed something good and pure in your life."

My cell vibrated, and I answered the call. "Winwood."

"Hello, Officer, this is Gemma. I'm Joe's sister."

"Gemma, hey. Is everything okay?"

She exhaled noisily. "He's doing well. Some of his memories are coming back; he seems steadier, wants to go back to work. Can you believe that?"

Yeah, I could. "He's dedicated."

"Yeah, well, he said something that I wanted to tell you, and it didn't make much sense at first, and I don't want to bother you."

I flicked the phone to speaker and held it between me and Mack. "Go on?"

"He said that the photo from the board had bank passwords on the back, something he used to do to keep it secret. Does that make sense? I mean, I get he shouldn't have done that, but it is what it is."

"Passwords. Okay."

"He said Heloise knew where they were, that you needed to talk to her."

"Thank you."

"He also said it didn't matter about those passwords,

because he thought he'd spotted errors in the bank statements, so he'd changed them all."

Fuck. He'd changed codes; Heloise had been locked out? So she couldn't do her skimming? Well, that explained the break-in, if Periapsis was looking for replacement passwords.

"Thank you, Gemma. That's very helpful. We'll come in at some point and get a full statement."

"Thank you, Detective."

I ended the call, and Mack and I exchanged knowing glances. "Passwords, eh? Cops 1, Heloise 0," Mack observed.

"Yep."

He fist pumped, then grinned at me. "You hungry?"

"Starved."

"Cool, I'll go get us some burritos from down the street."

"Sounds good."

I watched him jog off as the sun warmed the top of my head. I sighed as a flickering memory of last night with Oliver played out in my thoughts. I was free now to date him openly, if he still wanted that kind of thing. Fuck knew what I would do to win him over. My knowledge of romantic words and deeds was zero. I'd probably fuck this up before it even had a chance of really taking off, but in for a penny… as the old folks say.

I yanked my phone out of my front pocket. A gum wrapper fell to the sidewalk, then blew away in a gust of hot air. I dialed Oliver's number, my gut a mishmash of anxiety and excitement.

"Hey," he said after picking up.

"Hey yourself."

"You sound raspy. Are you getting a cold?"

"No, I'm just… I have something in my throat. Exhaust probably. I'm outside waiting for Mack to bring us some food. First time I'll have eaten today."

"That's not good. A machine needs fuel to run."

That made me chuckle and feel oddly fuzzy inside. The man was preaching to me about unhealthy habits. Like my sister. Like someone who cared. The thing in my throat got thicker.

"Yep, and this machine will be running on burritos soon. The other thing that I wanted to tell you was that I recused myself from your case, citing a conflict of interest."

A long beat of dead silence followed. Fear that I had fucked things up already blossomed in my belly.

"So, we can date now?"

"Yeah, we can; I mean, if you want…"

"Oh, trust me, Detective, I *want*."

If I'd not been a chonky-ass cop, I'd have floated away on those gusty Cali winds.

Chapter Fifteen

Oliver

I WAS GOING ON A DATE.

Tonight.

With Jackson.

Jamie perched on the edge of my bed while Daisy and Scarlett rummaged through my closet, their enthusiasm barely contained, transforming my bedroom into a chaotic council of fashion.

"Daddy, wear the blue shirt! It makes your eyes look nice," Scarlett insisted, holding up a shirt that had seen better days.

"Is this a jeans place, or a slacks place, or should you be in your Armani?" Jamie asked for the third time. "Are you sure you don't want me to message him?" Finally, he picked up my phone and waggled it.

"He said casual is okay."

"Armani can be casual," Jamie smirked. Asshole. This from the man who wore waistcoats to go grocery shopping. To underscore that, he tugged at the paisley one he was wearing now, with jeans, and assumed a pose.

"Armani is for games and traveling," I groused, and he snorted a laugh.

"Wear your nice jeans, not the ones with the paint," Daisy added, her tone suggesting that my usual non-hockey attire might not be up to par for whatever Jackson had planned. "And not your hockey stuff."

"Okay, not hockey, got it."

There was an awful lot of LA Storm purple piled on the side shelves, most of it in plastic still, but it was all splashed with my name and number, and while I wasn't a Hollywood celeb, I didn't want to be noticed, unless people really looked.

I stood there, amidst a sea of clothing choices, feeling an odd mix of excitement and unease. The date with Jackson loomed large in my mind, overshadowing even the simplest decisions. I stared at the clothes, unable to muster the energy to make a choice, my thoughts a whirlwind of anticipation and nerves, and I felt suddenly overwhelmed and lethargic.

Jamie, ever observant, watched me with a concerned frown. "Oliver, you okay? You've been staring at that shirt for five minutes now."

I blinked, pulled from my reverie. "Yeah, I'm fine. Just… can't decide, I guess."

But Jamie wasn't convinced. "When's the last time you checked your sugar?" he asked, his voice carrying an edge of worry.

"I'm not in a hypo," I murmured and picked up a discarded shirt in pale green.

"You haven't checked your watch in all the time I've been in the room."

"Hmmm?"

Jamie's concern deepened. "I think you should check it now. You're looking a bit off, mate." He grabbed my hand and pulled back my sleeve, and I tried to recall the last time I'd glanced at it. The day had been a blur of preparations and excitement for the evening ahead.

"Jesus, Oli, that's high, right?"

I focused on the numbers—they didn't seem right—and I blinked at them.

"Oli?" He was off the bed now, cradling my face. "Did you inject for the cookie you ate earlier?"

"I think so… Damn," I muttered, realization dawning. The cookie tasting. Jamie, Daisy, and Scarlett had spent the afternoon baking, a fun distraction that had turned into an impromptu taste test for me. I'd indulged in a cookie, caught up in the moment and the laughter, and fuck—had I really forgotten to adjust my insulin afterward? That wasn't me. I was rigidly controlled and I never forgot my insulin. Yet, here I was, so caught up in the prospect of my date with Jackson, I'd let it slip and now my sugar was high and my eyesight was blurring.

I picked up my phone to dial in the insulin, but Jamie stopped me. "How about you check manually as well, yeah?"

Nodding, I retrieved my glucose meter from the nightstand, a sense of unease growing. The girls were used to me pricking my finger and waited for the reading, still discussing blue jeans over black, and I didn't have to wait long for the reading. The number flashed on the screen, confirming Jamie's suspicion and the figures on my watch:

my sugar levels were high, much higher than they should be.

Fucking great.

Jamie stood up, his expression softening. "Hey, it's okay. Just dial in what you need now, and you'll be right as rain by the time Jackson picks you up."

The girls nodded. "We can help pick your outfit while you take care of that," Daisy offered, her voice earnest, and yet more clothes came out of the closet.

Jamie patted my arm, then went to a crouch in front of the growing pile, chatting to Daisy about what slacks were, and I administered the insulin, feeling foolish for letting my excitement disrupt my routine. As the insulin began to work, the lethargy started to lift, replaced by a renewed sense of anticipation for the evening, and also regret that I'd fucked up. Any expert would tell me that these things happened, but they didn't to me. I was an elite athlete, albeit getting on in athlete-years, and the team doc would have a fit if he thought for a moment I was letting real life interfere with my health.

He should try living with diabetes and see what it was like to have it so much a part of life.

I shook off the negatives, and with the crisis averted, Jamie and the girls rallied around me, helping me select the perfect outfit. A newer blue shirt and "*nice black jeans*" were the unanimous choice, and as I dressed, I couldn't help but smile at my girls.

"Okay, how do I look?" I asked, turning to face them.

"You look great, Daddy!" Scarlett exclaimed, while Daisy nodded vigorously.

Jamie clapped me on the back. "Jackson won't know

what hit him." Then, he gathered the girls to him and made a duck face as he captured a selfie with me in the background. I never even had time to pose. He snickered as he pocketed his cell and herded the girls downstairs. A message from him flashed on my phone with the photo and a message a minute later.

> Jamie: Don't make too much noise when you do the walk of shame.

He added an eggplant, and the raindrop emoji, and I shook my head.

> Oliver: Fuck off

> Jamie: GASP! I'm horrified at your lack of language skills.

> Oliver: Fuck off again

At least I was smiling, and the nerves had eased. I hadn't dated since I'd met Melissa, which was god knows how many years ago, but I couldn't worry about that now as I checked my bag. Backup insulin, needle, pump, testing kit—all in case the system I was wearing now let me down—phone, wallet, keys. Some days, I wished I could just walk out of the house as I was, but something new—like a date, possibly more physical things—and I had to cover all contingencies. Last in was the small container of Skittles to give me an instant sugar boost if I needed it. Then I was done. It was five minutes to seven, and he'd be here soon.

I didn't know what to do, so I flopped onto the bed, staring at the photos next to me. It was Melissa and me on our last vacation in Vancouver. She was pregnant with Daisy, and I was holding Scarlett, smiling so damn hard.

"What am I doing?" I asked the beautiful woman in the photo, and I didn't expect a reply, and I wasn't sure about an afterlife, but what if she was watching now? "I still love you," I whispered to the empty room, "but I think you'd like Jackson. He's all gritty and grumpy and sexy. I'm sorry you're not here, Mel." Grief curled in my chest, and I had to breathe through it. "I'm so sorry."

"He's here," Jamie murmured from the door, and I snapped around to face him, almost tumbling off the bed before standing. "It's okay, you know," he added, then brushed down my shirt as if I had lint all over it. "She wanted you to be happy."

I caught his hand, and he didn't tug it away. "I feel like I'm betraying what we had."

Jamie hugged me then, this slip of a Brit who seemed to know what to do and when. "It's not a betrayal when she gave you permission to live and love."

I nodded, hugged him tight, and we stood back as he casually checked me from head to toe.

"Go get him, Cowboy," he said in his best approximation of my Texas drawl, which he'd clearly learned from Dallas re-runs because it was horrific.

"You still suck at that accent," I said in my best upper-class Brit.

He faked shock. "You just butchered the King's English," he gasped.

Then, laughing, we headed downstairs to find Jackson sitting on the bottom step, Daisy on his lap, and Scarlett cross-legged on the floor, listening as he read to them. He stopped when he heard us, and glanced back, his jade eyes bright, his stubble gone as if he'd shaved it for me, and his pink lips curved in a smile. He still looked tired, but so gorgeous.

"Hey," he said and scooped up Daisy before standing and placing her on the floor.

"Hey," I replied, because yep, that was about all I could manage.

The girls giggled, Jamie freaking giggled, the ass, and then, with a flurry of goodbye kisses, hugs, and warnings for Daisy and Scarlett to be good for Jamie, we left. As soon as the door shut us out, Jackson stepped into my space, tilted my chin, and kissed me deeply.

It was a hello and a promise, all rolled into one.

"Hey," he said again, and this time his voice was deeper, sexier.

"Hey."

He escorted me to his car, a classic Buick Riviera that'd seen better days but was clean inside. "I know we could take your Ferrari," he began.

I frowned. "I don't have a Ferrari."

He faked shock. "That's a game changer," he deadpanned, then opened the freaking door for me with a flourish. "I was only going to date you if you had a Ferrari."

I stopped him with a hand on his arm as concern flooded me. Was he being serious? A hard knot started in my chest, and maybe my tone was off, but I had to get this out. "Most of my money is in trust for the girls. The rest goes to... other things. After hospital costs for Melissa's care when she was ill, I didn't have much. I don't have a fancy mansion or a Ferrari. I'm not rich."

His eyes widened. "I was joking," he said, and for a moment, I thought I'd fucked up, because deep down, I knew what we had was a firestorm of attraction and nothing to do with who I was, or who he was.

We were just us.

Shit. I'd overreacted, and now he'd tell me to fuck off, and I didn't want the date to end before it had even begun. "Sorry, I have—"

He kissed me to stop me talking and then guided me to get into the car. "You can trust me," he said. He belted himself into the driver's seat, then turned to face me, and in a perfect copy of my accent, he drawled: "I'm the law."

Fuck. That was hot.

And great, now I'm hard in my best black jeans.

JACKSON PARKED IN A SHADOWED ALLEYWAY, THE KIND OF place I would have thought twice about if I were alone, even if I was a big burly hockey defenseman. But with Jackson, it felt like an adventure as he led me to the nondescript back door of an Italian restaurant, pushing it open with the ease of someone who'd done it many times before. The warm smell of garlic and herbs wafted out, inviting us in.

There was no greeting with menus or the usual fanfare of being seated at a table. Instead, a young man, who couldn't have been over seventeen, approached us with a bottle of wine. His movements were precise, a certain meticulousness in the way he placed the bottle on our table in a far corner of the room, and he wouldn't meet our gaze.

"No menus," he stated simply, a slight smile playing on his lips. "Food will be out quick-quick." His tone was direct and to the point, and I thanked him as he left.

I raised an eyebrow at Jackson, curious about this unconventional setup with the wine and no menus. He leaned in, his voice low. "That's Alessandro. He's on the spectrum. Couple of months back, Mack and I met him wandering in a park, completely bewildered. We walked him home, and well, according to his family, that means we're practically family now."

Before I could ask more, another man emerged from the kitchen, wiping his hands on an apron adorned with the colors of the Italian flag. He was a sturdy figure, with a warmth in his eyes that spoke of a life spent around food and family. When he spotted Jackson, his face lit up with a genuine affection. Jackson stood, so I did too.

The man enveloped him in a hearty hug. "Jackson, my boy!" he boomed, releasing him before turning his attention to me.

"This is my date, Oliver," Jackson introduced us, and I got a hug as big as Jackson had gotten.

"Welcome! I'm Franco," he declared, as if his name was an afterthought. "Welcome to our little slice of Italy, served family-style, with the freshest and finest options available. I'll be back soon!"

The conversation flowed easily from there, Jackson regaling me with stories of his work, nothing awful, the quirky funny thoughts, and in return, I told him some about me being traded here with the girls in tow. We didn't discuss Melissa anymore—I guess she wouldn't have liked me fixating on her while I was supposed to find a new kind of happy.

Alessandro returned intermittently, each time bringing dishes more aromatic and enticing than the last: fresh bruschetta on toasted homemade bread, pasta that melted in your mouth, meats seasoned and cooked to perfection. I picked what I could eat and injected as best I could, and it was wonderful food and good company.

When Alessandro brought out desserts, he hovered after he placed them down. "I did this one," he said, gesturing at the concoction of berries and cream.

I took a taste and grinned up at him. "Perfect."

"He rescued me," Alessandro added and pointed at Jackson.

"You were so brave, and you rescued yourself," Jackson corrected him, and Alessandro blushed as he left.

"What exactly happened?" I asked when it was the two of us again.

"Mack and I were heading out to a scene, but they kept us back, so we were on a break, and this kid just comes over to us and tells us he's lost. He'd been hovering for a while, uncertain. Just as I was about to go ask him if he was okay, he asked us for help. He's a good kid. Quirky. Sweet. Hell, walking him home, that was nothing," Jackson said, brushing off the act as mundane. "But the gratitude from his family, you'd think we'd saved the world."

Franco, passing by, nodded vigorously. "You *did* save our world that day," he insisted. "Alessandro's a special boy, and not everyone takes the time to see that. But,

Jackson, you and your partner, you saw him. You helped him. That makes you family."

As we finished our meal, Franco refused any attempt at payment, and Jackson left a huge tip that more than covered it instead, with me adding in some as well. Then, walking back to the car, we held hands, and I felt a connection to Jackson that went beyond the surface.

"Tonight was… it was so good, Jackson. Thank you for sharing that with me," I said.

Jackson smiled, that same soft smile that had drawn me in from the start. "I'm glad you enjoyed it. Let's get you home."

We buckled up, and then I held out a hand, which he took, feeling a hundred kinds of awkward and almost shy. "I'm not ready for the date to end."

"I'm so glad you said that."

"You want to get a coffee or something?"

"I have coffee at my place." He quirked an eyebrow.

"Then, how about a coffee at your place?"

"I can get us home in twenty," he said.

And not that I was watching the clock, but he made it in eighteen.

Chapter Sixteen

Jackson

NOT THAT I WAS IN A HURRY OR ANYTHING, BUT I WAS IN A hurry.

Oliver was all mine for a few hours. No kids, no hockey, no criminal activities.

God, please, by all that is holy, do not let someone call me with something work-related. I know I'm a public servant and all that, but Lord, I do like this man and want to get laid. So, if it's in your wheelhouse, and we all know it probs is, give my overworked ass one night of peace. Amen.

We pulled up in front of my complex with undue haste, the slip and slide into my end parking slot pulling a raised brow from Oliver.

"That's known as the Starsky and Hutch skid and park. It's taught at the police academy," I explained as I shifted the Buick into Park, then cut the engine.

"Oh, really? What else do they teach at the academy that's from old cop shows?"

"Well, there was this class on how to kiss someone you really want to fuck."

He chuckled. "Do tell."

"Much rather show."

I reached for him, hand cupping the back of his neck, and pulled his mouth to mine. Unlike today's cars, my baby has a split bench that allows two grown men to get at each other with no damn console in the way. Yay, Detroit, in the seventies, knew what they were doing. Big cars, big engines, big seats.

His lips were soft, pliant, and opened over mine. I slid my tongue into his mouth, sighing dreamily as the taste of Oliver and Italian food exploded on my taste buds. The kiss was messy and so fucking hot. We had to break apart, breathless, to find, then pop our seatbelt latches.

"Ahh, there we go," I purred, grabbing at him with greedy fingers, only to see him easing out of the car.

Shit. I exited as well. Oliver smiled at me over the roof. "Let's go inside. If we stay out here much longer, we'll be doing it in the front seat, and that'll be uncomfortable for both of us."

He was right. Neither of us were what you would call pocket-sized. I jangled my keys, took his hand, and led him to the breezeway for my small unit. We climbed the stairs to my second-floor apartment, the wail of a far-off siren mixing in with the muffled sounds of life in the city. He followed quietly, the metal stairs creaking under our weight as we climbed. Outside my door, I paused, a rush of unease creeping up my spine. I stalled short of sliding my key into the lock.

"We don't have to do this if you don't want to," Oliver said from behind me.

I shook my head, eyes on the small nameplate on my door. It used to read *Jackson Winwood,* but some punk kids had scribbled my name out and written *Oink-Oink Pig Residence,* which had made me snicker. So I'd left it. Not that anyone ever came here anyway, so what difference did it make? Suddenly it made all kinds of a difference that I was mortified to admit.

"I'm not the tidiest man," I confessed and got a little pat on the ass.

"I'm not here to look at your dusty tables, Jackson. I'm here to fuck you."

A shiver of anticipation danced along my skin. Knowing the inside of my place was depressing as shit, I braced myself, then began unbolting the locks. Sure, people knew a cop lived here, but that didn't mean they wouldn't rob me. Probably my status as a detective upped the chances of me being burgled.

Once the door was free, I reached around to the right, flipped on the sole light, and headed in.

"It's a bachelor pad," I said and got a smile. Then he stepped inside. The smile slipped for a second before he had it back in place. "Sorry. I… no one ever comes here. It's too… well, I don't like my place much. Just… sit down on the couch and give me… I didn't think we'd end up here or I would have… cleaned the place?"

"Jackson, it's fine, honestly," he lied. I knew it wasn't fine. The place was a rathole, and I was the king rat. Sure, I had a housekeeper who did the basics, but a fast vacuum couldn't cover the air of no shits being given clinging to the smoke-stained walls.

"My housekeeper does vacuum and dust." I moved around the place, picking up magazines, a few milk cartons, and a bag of old takeout. I chose to ignore the empty bottles strewn all over, even though I was sure Oliver had eyeballed them and found me lacking. "She's not been in for a few weeks. Her son just had a baby, so she's spending a couple of months with them."

I booted an empty beer bottle under the sofa. Oliver moved to me, his gaze penetrating.

"I know it's lacking compared to your house, but—"

He closed the distance in one step. His hands rose to cup my face and his lips—oh, those sinful lips—touched on mine. Once, twice, thrice.

"Your place is fine."

I rolled my eyes as my fingers slid around his waist to grasp his beefy ass.

"Liar," I whispered, then licked my way into his mouth.

Worries about the sad state of my home drifted away as we made out languidly, exploring, teasing...

"Where's the bedroom?" he asked when we broke apart.

I rolled my hips. His cock and mine met. A moan rumbled out of both of us.

"It's right this way."

I stole one more kiss, then gave him a soft shove in the right direction. He snagged my arm, tugging me along into my stuffy bedroom. Again, only the barest necessities greeted us. A dresser, a bed, and a window where my dead orchid sat on the sill. Planted by my double bed, we came back together, this time with more passion. Fingers yanked and pulled on buttons and zippers. I kissed his neck, then freed him from his shirt, kissing each inch of skin revealed before lust took over. I began nibbling, stroking, palming. His dick, his balls, his tight pucker.

"Fuck, I'm too close already," Oliver grunted when I toyed with his hole, his strong legs spread wide. "Lie down."

"Bossy bastard. You lie down."

His dark eyes grew hotter. I kicked off my pants and briefs, then embraced him, our cocks swaying as a moment of swordplay broke out. When he was absorbed in the battle of the dicks, I placed my hands on his pecs and pushed. He hit the bed. The headboard slamming into the wall. I had some doubts that my old frame would hold up to the workout it was about to get.

"The sheets smell like you," he said as I pounced on him like a starving canine stumbling over a rare steak. My mouth slanted over his as he moved me to my back with a slick wrestling move. When I was looking up at him in the light of a streetlamp outside my window, I gazed at perfection. His beautiful eyes, strong jaw, thick neck, powerful shoulders…

"You're the most gorgeous man that I have ever seen," I whispered, awed that someone so sinfully splendid was about to lie with me. Me. Jackson Winwood.

"No, that title goes to you."

He lowered his head to kiss me, his arms locked. I threw my legs around him, my heels resting on his ass. His hips gyrated, cock rubbing over cock, his leaking head spreading his pre-cum over my slick head. I carded my fingers into his hair, sucked on his tongue, and began saying silly things to him that I had never said to any other man. Flowery compliments about his nose, his eyebrows, his lips. We moved back and forth, him pressing me into the mattress, then me moving atop him. All the while, our dicks were throbbing hot shafts, leaving glistening trails across our thighs, bellies, and hips.

When he had me on my back, hands pinned over my head, he moved just so. The head of his cock slid downward, under my balls, and settled there. I was mindless with lust at this point, unwilling to dither around trying to assert dominance any longer. His hips flickered. His fat cockhead pressed against my hole.

"Fuck me," I gasped, arching up off the bed to try to get him inside me. All pretense was gone. I needed to be fucked. I needed to fuck him. "Lube and condoms… drawer… dresser."

"Stay there, do not move." He left the bed, raced to my dresser, and upended two drawers of socks and underwear, searching. "You asshole. You could tell me which drawer they're in."

"Nah, it's way more fun to lie here with my prick in my hand and enjoy the sights." And what a sight it was. That bubble butt of his was all kinds of delicious-looking. I had wild plans to spread those meaty cheeks, then spear him with my cock over and over until he begged me to come inside him.

He laughed, then found what he was searching for in my T-shirt drawer. I enjoyed the sight of him returning to me, the tube of lube in one hand, rope of condoms in the other.

"Just for making me search, I'm going to fuck you twice as long," he announced as he kneeled beside me.

"Your threats need work, Cowboy," I said, my gaze roaming over him, then stopping at the small white patch on his biceps. "Are you good?"

He gave me the oddest look. "I like to think so."

It took me a second. "Oh, no, not… no, I wasn't asking if you were a good fuck. I meant with your sugar and all. Are you good? Do we need to get some food or something in here? Candy or something. No, candy is bad. Right?"

Shit, I really needed to hone up on my diabetic knowledge. Oliver, being a great guy, kissed me senseless, worked his thigh between mine, and found my opening with two thick, slick fingers.

"I'm good, but thanks for asking, and worrying."

My body thrummed with want as he began to work me open, his fingers spreading wide, then twisting time and again.

"Don't want you… to pass out… crucial moment. Fuck! Christ. Shit. Damn, that is… right there. Yeah, candy is dandy, but a prostate tickle is quicker." He chortled at my ramblings. "I'm punch drunk for cock. Get inside me, Oliver."

"You cops are so bossy," he said, tsked, and moved over me. I rested a foot on his shoulder, and one on his lower back, as he pushed into me. The burn was intense. "Breathe, baby."

"I am… breathing. Your cock… is enormous."

"Flattery will get you thoroughly ransacked," he

huffed, eased out, and then moved back in. This happened time and again, each thrust in a little deeper until he was buried to the hilt. "Breathe, baby, just breathe."

I loved the sound of that word rushing out of him as he battled to maintain control. *Baby.* I'd never been anyone's baby before. I arched up, then clenched. He trembled, growled, and then began giving me the ransacking he'd promised. The man had tremendous stamina. His legs were strong, powering him like twin pistons that pumped endlessly. My flagging cock sprang back into life when his fat cockhead found my prostate. Windless and senseless from the fucking I was getting, I whimpered and whined, gasped and groaned. Somehow, in the fury of our joining, I managed to get a hand on my cock. The other was above my head, keeping my skull from kissing my thrift shop headboard.

The room was thick with the sounds and scents of sex. Oliver was purposeful off the ice, just as he was on it. Sweat ran to the tip of his nose, then fell to my chest. That was what pushed me over. The sight of his perspiration dropping to my sweaty pectoral. I cried out something, no clue what, as a fire lit at the base of my spine. My balls contracted, my dick swelled, and I tumbled into the light. Cum pulsed out of me, coating my fingers and speckling my belly.

"So pretty. That's it, come for me, baby," Oliver ground out while pushing in for one final soul-searing thrust. His head snapped back as he came. A glorious sight I hoped I got to witness for years to come.

Yeah, I was greedy. And so head over heels nuts over this man that I dared to dream of a future together. Me.

Jackson Winwood. Had fallen in love. The man who couldn't manage to keep a freaking plant alive was daring to fantasize about something as emotionally demanding as a—*GULP!*—relationship. What did I know about such things? Emotions required nurturing. They needed to be watered weekly with love, fertilized with respect, and given access to sunny windows. I tended to bring out the opposite of tender feelings in most people, got my liquid nutrition from a Wild Turkey bottle, and spent most of my time in the darkness with seedy people doing illegal things. I'd kill any kind of decent, normal relationship faster than Van Helsing would stake a vampire.

"Are you okay?" Oliver asked, his words heated puffs tickling my face.

"Yeah, no, good… best I've been in… fuck, forever I think," I admitted, the candid reply easing the look of concern. "Kiss me?"

"Gladly," he replied, lowering his mouth to mine as he eased out, and I knew the moment of intimacy and revelations had passed. "I need to…"

He waved at his latex-sheathed cock as he moved to the side.

"Oh right, the bathroom is across the hall. Can't miss it. Only room in the place with a crapper."

He stole one final kiss, then left me lying in my bed, ass tender, heart and mind befuddled. I eased up to a sitting position, keeping my sight on his glorious ass until he entered my tiny bathroom and closed the door. Funny how guys who'd been as intimate as us could still feel funny taking a leak in front of the other. Jittery now that the easy stuff was over, I got up, winced at the twang in my sore hole, and found the nearest dirty shirt to wipe the cooling spunk off my belly. Yeah, the sex stuff, that was easy. Hormone-driven, cock in the lead, no need to feel anything other than pleasure.

But the ball of whatever it was in my chest right now? Hell, that was tougher. This wad of emotion was the hardest thing ever, and it terrified me right down to my cells.

"Hey, are you sure you're okay? I called your name a few times," Oliver asked, his arms coming around me from behind. I started. He smelled of lime-green soap. His chest was toasty warm against my chilling back.

My first reaction was to make some sort of asshole wisecrack about how his enormous cock had left me senseless. And while that was true to an extent—although my bunghole was wishing it could claim to be numb—that was covering up where my head really was.

I melted into his arms, sighing like a spring debutante, and tried this once to be open.

"I was caught up in the feelings that I'm feeling." He kissed my bare shoulder as I held my tacky tee to my thundering heart. "Wow, that was lame. I won't be putting Bob Dylan out of work as a lyricist anytime soon."

"I think what you said was beautiful, Jackson," he whispered as he pressed tiny little pecks along my shoulder and neck. My eyes flickered shut when he held me close. "I'm not exactly a poet either. I knock people down for a living. I'm feeling a lot of feelings right now too, if that helps."

"It does," I confessed, inhaling the unique blend of my

soap and Oliver's skin as the aroma enveloped me. "You think we could maybe do more of this?"

"Fucking? Oh yeah."

That made me chuckle. "No, well, yes, fucking obviously, because I need to get my dick into that sweet ass of yours sometime soon, but the other things like this, too. This right here is about as perfect a moment as I have ever experienced with another human being. Just being loved, sated, held firm in your arms…" I paused to blink away some kind of huge feeling threatening to make me weepy. No one wanted that. Crying and cops? Nope, not going to happen. "I'd like to do more of this dating and embracing after sex stuff."

"Cuddling?" he teased, then tugged on my earlobe with his teeth.

"Oh please, as if a cop and a hockey player would ever cuddle." I turned to gaze upon him, capturing his face between my hands, and kissed him soundly on the lips. "Maybe we can call it lounging. Yeah, lounging. Sounds like something two macho dudes would do. We can lounge after having sex."

"You're a total idiot."

He wrapped his arms around my middle, then used his hip in some sort of slick wrestling move to topple my not-so-tiny self to my bed. We grappled for a minute or two, me trying to use all the self-defense moves I had learned at the academy to free myself from his grip until I realized that being in his grip was kind of turning me on. My dick was half hard, resting snugly under his balls as he sat on my pelvis, smirking down at me in victory.

"If we had the lube, you could sit on my dick and ride me like a mustang, Cowboy," I said, my voice gravelly.

His expression changed from amused to aroused in the blink of an eye. "Let me find it," he said, and my dick grew another inch. "You know, I think I might be falling for you," he added.

"Yeah?" This sounded like dangerous territory. Was he really ready for this?

"Even though I have all these memories in my head, it's like Melissa is telling me... I'm falling hard," he added, and his skin pinkened.

"I think—" From somewhere not in the bed, the sound of a cell phone ringing sliced into the night like a shiv. It was Mack. The ringtone was unmistakable. "Fuck," I huffed, fully prepared to ignore it. Let someone else take the call. Maybe the two new guys that had just started could go play with the gangland lords and Mafia dons this once. All the play left Oliver's eyes, and he slid off me, lube in hand, dick fat and hard, to look at me sprawled in my bed unmoving.

"That's you," he said. I nodded. "Aren't you going to answer it?"

I huffed in exasperation, still debating if I could somehow not see what my partner wanted at ten minutes past midnight.

"Sometimes, I hate my fucking job," I snarled as I rolled from the bed to find my phone. When I located my pants, I nearly tore the back pocket off in my pique. "Mack, this had better be fucking important," I growled into the phone instead of hello.

"It is. It's Lazlo Richter, the receptionist at the clinic.

Someone knocked the security guy out and tied him up, and hell, the kid's just been admitted to the Holy Trinity ER with a gunshot wound."

"The fuck? I thought we'd closed this down."

"It looks bad, Jackson."

"I… yeah, be right there." I ended the call just as Oliver padded into view, still clutching the lube, still looking like every dream I had ever dreamed. Fuck this fucking world. "Hey, Oliver, so something has happened…"

Chapter Seventeen

Oliver

THE SHIFT FROM INTIMACY TO CHAOS WAS JARRING. LYING there with Jackson, I felt my world was good, and I'd even used the L word, until his phone shattered the silence. I'd watched the change in Jackson's expression as he listened to the voice on the other end, the tension in his jaw, the sudden hardness in his eyes. When he hung up, his gaze met mine, heavy with a weight he seemed unsure how to share.

"Lazlo got shot, and someone tied up the security guard," he finally said, his voice low, the words hitting me like a physical blow. Lazlo was always eager to help, always with a smile ready, despite the chaos he sometimes faced. It made little sense.

"What?"

"I know I'm off this case, but…" He stared at me for a moment. "I have to go."

"Of course, I get it, I—"

"I need to take you home," he said, already up and getting dressed.

I scrambled to follow, yanking on my wrinkled shirt as my mind raced with questions and a sinking feeling of dread.

"I want to come with you," I began, but he pressed a finger to my lips and shook his head. There was so much unspoken in that moment. It wasn't my place to rush to a crime scene. I wasn't a cop. This was a friend of mine. This was something to do with the clinic, but worse was that if I went, I might compromise something. "I wish I could go with you," I amended, and couldn't help feeling sidelined when it mattered most.

In his car, the conversation shifted rapidly to Lazlo's condition, the senseless violence, and what it might mean for the clinic. Each question I posed seemed to weigh heavier on Jackson, his responses short, tinged with anger and resolve. He couldn't tell me anything, and the last thing he needed was me asking anything.

When we reached my gate, he unbuckled his seatbelt as I did mine, then dragged me over to him, kissing me deeply and holding me tight as if he never wanted to let me go. The kiss felt like a promise, but it was also me asking him to stay safe.

Then, he was gone, leaving me in the dark, both literally and metaphorically.

Standing there, watching the taillights disappear, I felt a mix of emotions. Concern for Lazlo, frustration at being left behind, and a nagging fear for Jackson's safety. The night that had started with such promise had taken a dark turn, leaving me upside-down. I punched in the gate code, then waited until it closed behind me before trudging up to the house.

Back inside, the familiar sounds of the *Great British Baking Show* filled the living room and Jamie was there, his long frame stretched out on the sofa, a cup of tea in hand, completely absorbed in the show. The normalcy of the scene felt almost jarring.

As soon as I walked in, Jamie's attention snapped to me, his relaxed demeanor changing instantly as he scrambled to his feet. "Back already? Shit, you look knackered?" he blurted out, ready to spring into action. "What did hot-cop do?"

I slumped to the other end of the sofa, and Jamie must have seen something in my expression because he paused, then his gaze shifted, landing somewhere on my throat. His eyes narrowed, and a smirk slowly spread across his face as he pressed a hand to his neck. "Hmm, is that a birthmark? Or did Jackson take a bite out of you?"

Horrified, I reached up to cover the mark, feeling my face heat.

"So, I take it you did the nasty?" he poked, but I couldn't bring myself to banter. "Oli? You're worrying me. If you're home, then where's the cop, and why do you look like death warmed over?"

"Shit, J," I muttered and bent over my knees, my chest tight.

"Was he terrible in bed?" Jamie teased, but his tone was filled with concern.

"No," I said, though my voice sounded weak.

Jamie's expression softened as he took in my state, the jesting falling away. "Ollie, mate, talk to me. You look like you've been through the wringer."

His concern was genuine, and the events of the night

replayed in my mind. Each minute with Jackson, the call about Lazlo, the sudden and stark end to the evening, I kept going over every moment.

"Someone shot one of the staff at the clinic—Jackson had to leave, and he gave me a ride back."

"What? Who?"

"Lazlo."

"The young guy at reception?"

"Yeah, he's a good kid. Young, motivated, and he loves working there, and I was only talking to him a few days ago." I closed my eyes and covered them with my hands. "Someone's shot him."

The room fell silent except for the muffled voices on the TV. Something about raspberry and white chocolate and one presenter wearing a floppy hat. What that had to do with baking I didn't know, but Jamie and the girls loved this show. Jamie's hand landed on my shoulder, a silent message of support, and he squeezed.

"Christ, Oli, that's rough." Jamie's voice was low, the usual playful edge gone.

I nodded, feeling the full weight of the evening. I dropped my hands and opened my eyes, meeting Jamie's gaze. "I don't understand it, Jamie. The clinic, it's a haven, a place that's supposed to be above all the… the violence and darkness of the streets. Lazlo, he's just like Joe, someone who wants to make things better."

"Was he shot at the clinic?" Jamie asked, and I had to admit, I didn't know.

"I guess so. Jackson said the security guy had been knocked out, so yeah, the clinic, Jackson wouldn't tell me anything."

"It could have been a drive-by." Jamie shuddered. "I've lived in the US for eight years, and I still don't get the gun thing," he murmured. Then he shook his head, his expression grim. "Some people want to watch the world burn. Doesn't matter who gets caught in the flames."

The bitterness in his tone matched the helplessness I felt. Lazlo, with his whole life ahead of him, suffered, and now, the man I loved was out there trying to fix the broken things.

The man I loved.

"I told Jackson I was falling for him," I whispered.

Jamie blinked at me, then muted the TV. "Really?"

"I still have Melissa in here." I pressed a hand to my heart. "And sometimes I have these dreams and she's telling me she wants me to be happy, but it all seems impossible."

"Aww, Oli," Jamie sighed. "I know it isn't easy, but Melissa was all about love, and she'd want you to find someone to make you happy."

"I know."

"And does this idiot cop of yours make you happy?"

"Yeah."

Jamie nodded in all seriousness, then grinned, poking his glasses up and punching me in the arm.

"Go, Oli!" he said, and gave me that awful fake-crowd noise he did whenever he celebrated. I'd noticed Scarlett did the same thing, absolutely besotted with her Uncle Jamie. Then, he curled on his side and picked up his tea, sipping it and wrinkling his nose. "Cold." He headed out to the kitchen, but stopped at the door. "Want a cuppa? Coffee?"

I pressed a hand to my belly. I felt nauseous.

"Water is good." I followed him out, added, "Give me five."

Heading upstairs, I checked on Daisy first. She was my chaos-girl, the covers everywhere, sprawled across the mattress, her hair in disarray, a book under one hand and her beloved Annie-bear tucked into her side. Annie-bear was something Melissa and I had given her when she was only a year old, a fluffy teddy with enormous amber eyes. Melissa kissed the bear every time Daisy asked her to. I made sure to kiss Annie-bear now, tucking her in with Daisy, then covering her with the quilt and pressing a similar kiss to my baby girl.

"Love you," I whispered.

"Daddy," she mumbled in her sleep, and my already full heart just expanded a little more. I'd do anything to keep her and Scarlett safe, and it hurt that they'd already lost their mom. What were Lazlo's parents thinking right now? Did they know? Were they scared? Was he still alive?

I shook away the thoughts, drew the door nearly closed, then headed to Scarlett's room. She was the neat sleeper, and her room was immaculate. The therapist we saw as a family after Melissa's diagnosis explained that this was partly about control, and mostly, the way Scarlett was. I crouched by her bed, taking in the face that was so much like Melissa's, and pressed a kiss to her forehead.

"Love you," I murmured and stroked the hair from her face.

I loved them so much. So, was there enough capacity in my heart for more love? Would I have to shift out some of the grief that still lived there to make space for Jackson? I had to do the right thing for my kids, and was bringing a cop into the house the right thing? What if someone shot him tonight while he was out? What if being a cop got him killed? Could my heart handle losing someone else? Could the kids handle losing another parental figure?

Was I getting ahead of myself?

With a sigh, I headed back downstairs, catching the time on the wall clock. Why did it feel as if days had passed?

Because everything had changed.

"We need to talk about this falling for the cop thing," Jamie said when I was back in the kitchen.

"Nothing much to say," I said, and Jamie rolled his eyes.

"Sit. I want to hear everything."

So, I told him, and he smiled, and by the time I went to bed, he'd managed to calm me down and make me see I hadn't fucked things up. Still, I didn't sleep well, and my first thoughts when I woke up were about Lazlo and Jackson. I scrambled for my phone to stop my alarm and saw a simple message.

> Jackson: L's okay. Security guard okay.
> Talk later X

I rapidly tapped out a reply.

> Oliver: Thank you for letting me know.
> Stay safe X

I loved that we both sent kisses, because somehow, in all of this, it meant something. Jamie and the girls were making breakfast, and I kissed and hugged both of my daughters before tousling Jamie's perfect hair and earning a growl.

"Leave it, you arsehole! I have a meeting for a research project." He wore a green waistcoat over a snowy white shirt. The waistcoat had gold-colored thread in a random pattern, and he rocked the style, embracing his eccentric Brit persona, complete with nerdy professor glasses. He looked like an academic dressed like this, and he was so damn clever. His area of specialty was math, but not just math—incomprehensible-to-anyone-normal math.

"Math?" I asked innocently, and Scarlett giggled.

"It's maths, and you know it," Jamie fake-snarled and passed me a mug of coffee.

"Math," I replied. "Right, girls?"

"Yep," Scarlett said, her smile widening.

"Maths, with an s, is short for mathematics, heathen," Jamie began with exaggerated patience and sipped his tea, his eyes bright with the familiar teasing. I needed this right now.

———

THE VIDEO ROOM WAS DIM, THE GLOW FROM THE SCREEN casting us all in a bluish light. Clips from the New York versus Carolina game flickered across it, showing New York's aggressive play and the decisive saves of their goalie. The guys were focused, analyzing the play-by-play, while Coach pointed out the strengths and how New York had exploited Carolina's weaknesses.

"They won this one because their goalie's on a hot

streak right now, but watch his left hand, there's a delay," one of the assistant coaches said, rewinding the footage to highlight the point.

I nodded along, but my mind was elsewhere, replaying the previous night's events. Lazlo's face, so full of life every time I saw him at the clinic, was now overshadowed by the news of the shooting. The reality of violence had shaken me more than I wanted to admit.

"Cowen!" Coach's voice cut through my thoughts, snapping me back to the present. "Mind joining us here?"

I straightened up, realizing I'd been called out. The room turned to me, waiting.

"Anything you want to add about their goalie?" Coach asked, his eyes sharp.

I quickly gathered myself, needing to lighten the mood and steer away from my distracted silence. "What, you mean, apart from his insane love of Milk Duds and a need to swim naked?" I quipped.

Laughter broke out, rippling through the room, a welcome release from the tension.

Coach shook his head, a smile tugging at his lips despite the attempt to stay serious. "All right, focus up. Let's use what we know; do you have anything useful?"

"Yeah, he gets cocky in the third period if NY is up by two," I added, and Coach nodded at me for that valuable insight.

As the session continued, I forced myself to concentrate, absorbing every play, every move. This was my team now, and if we were going to win against my former teammates, I needed to be fully present, to bring everything I had to the ice.

And not to think about falling in love, or Lazlo getting shot, or worrying about grief, or thinking the worst in every freaking scenario.

I had to stay in the present, and right now, that was hockey.

Still, that didn't stop me from staring at my phone when I got the chance.

Because I was falling hard, and it felt a lot like love.

Chapter Eighteen

Jackson

I SWEAR MY ASS WOULD SOON BE THE EXACT SHAPE OF A hospital waiting room chair. Mack and I spent endless hours waiting for victims to be allowed to speak to us. Thankfully, we were plainclothes, so we blended in better than our brothers and sisters in uniform while plunked down in a busy emergency room waiting area. If we kept our jackets on, no one could see our weapons and badges, and the tension that uniformed cops seated among the poorer and most vulnerable in our society sometimes drew was lessened.

No one told me I couldn't sit here and wait even though I was off the case, but one call to reorganize the rest of my day, and I wasn't moving an inch.

Mack had already spoken to Ian Brown, the security guard, who'd come out with a concussion and two stitches for a head wound, but given I wasn't officially on this case, I had to stand back. Ian didn't remember who'd hit him, or much at all, until he'd been found and brought into the hospital. I made a note to mention to Oliver that the clinic needed to check out the guys they hired to see if they were actually any good. Maybe I'd do it for him.

Mack was snoozing beside me as I people-watched, arms resting on my chest, legs stretched out and crossed at the ankle. We'd give Lazlo another hour to come out from under, then see if we could talk to him. Sometimes, that was dicey. The doctors weren't always keen on law enforcement showing up to question a victim. And I got it. But the sooner we could get the facts, the sooner we could move on things. The forensic investigators had been at the scene when Mack and I had arrived two hours ago, the clinic once again taped off with crime tape. I'd smiled sheepishly at Timothy. The man was pissed at me for blowing him off time after time. I was going to have to just stop playing him. I was with Oliver now. We'd not said a thing about exclusivity, but I didn't want anyone else. I'd never wanted to be with Timothy, but his flirtations had made me feel good, you know, attractive when I was not feeling at all that way.

Oliver filled that empty void in my chest now.

Oliver and the clinic. Man, what a clusterfuck things had become.

I wasn't sure if the place would survive another violent crime. If I had kids, I'd be damned if I'd take them to a facility where two people had been attacked within a month. Then again, many of the patients at the clinic had no other options. Joe and his staff treated everyone of every age, whether or not they had the means to pay. And while Joe was a good guy with a heart of gold, his bookkeeper, Heloise, had not been above milking the system.

"You want some coffee?" I asked Mack. He snored in reply. I tapped his forehead with the tip of my finger. He snorted awake, wiping awkwardly at the drool on his chin. "I said, you want some coffee?"

He blinked, then frowned. "No. Maybe. Okay." I gathered up the four empty cups on the end table beside me, got to my feet, and was glancing around for a trash can when a young doctor hustled out to us. He looked as tired as I felt. Guess cops and docs didn't get much sleep in this town.

"Mr. Richter is resting comfortably." I sighed in relief. The doc went on to tell us the basics before he grew a bit truculent. "He's willing to speak to you both, but I am restricting your time with him to five minutes. No more. And do not upset him."

We both nodded at the good doctor. He seemed less than pleased to be allowing two frumpy detectives into his world. We were given a long look before he left us to go help the next person on his long list of people in need.

"Okay, so technically, you're no longer on the case, so why don't you reach out to Timothy and see if he and his team have gotten a good match on the prints they lifted from the scene?"

"I promise I won't say a word," I wheedled as we made our way into the heart and soul of the ER. Since the wound was in the upper arm and had been clean—not hitting any bones or nerves—he'd been X-rayed, stitched up, and given some antibiotics and, probably, a tetanus shot. We saw a lot of shootings every year, and he'd probably not be admitted and would be released within a few hours. "I just want to hear what the man has to say."

"You just don't want to deal with Timothy," Mack countered, to which I shrugged. Yeah, I was a coward when it came to emotional anything. "Fine, but you just take notes and try to look like you didn't go twenty rounds with a demonic vacuum cleaner last night."

My fingers rose of their own accord to brush a tender spot on my neck. "You could have told me sooner. I'd have buttoned up and found a damn tie."

I tugged the neckline of my shirt up over my collarbone as my partner sniggered like a fool. "Asshole," I added just for flavor. We approached a nurses' station, asked about Lazlo, and were directed to a small room among about twenty. Moans filled the air. The smell of cleaner and iron were thick back here as doctors and nurses hustled from room to room purposefully.

Mack entered first. I followed, my sight touching on Lazlo as he sat on a gurney, his biceps bandaged, his face pale as snow. His gaze flickered to Mack, then to me, but he seemed reluctant to open the dialogue.

"We're glad to see that you're going to be okay, Mr. Richter," Mack opened, and I nodded silently, easing my phone out of the back pocket of my wrinkled trousers. "I know you're in a lot of pain, so we're going to make this brief so you can rest before you're discharged."

Lazlo glanced from Mack to me. "Detective Winwood is here to take notes."

"Can you tell Oliver that I'm okay? And tell him to tell Joe. I don't think I can work tomorrow, but maybe the day after?"

"I'll let Mr. Cowan know that you're going to be fine. And I am relatively sure that Dr. Baxter is not going to call you out over a missed shift or two when he's only just out of a hospital bed himself."

"He's out now?"

"Yep. Now you rest and recuperate. Being shot hurts."

"Yeah, seriously." Lazlo sighed as he cradled his wounded arm to his chest, a dark blue sling keeping the arm stationary. "I think I might know who the shooter was."

Mack glanced at me. I held up my phone. "Are you agreeable with us recording this conversation, Mr. Richter?" I asked and got a nod from Lazlo. If only every victim/witness were this cooperative, our work would be so much easier. The call for some doctor to report to a certain room floated by. I placed my cell on the rolling tray that held some ice chips in a cup, and a box of tissues. "Thank you. So, can you tell us why you were at the clinic so late at night? According to what the responding officers have in their report, you were working?"

"Yeah, it's the end of the month, and since we're so short-staffed, I was trying to get the billing done and sent to Heloise before she chewed my ass again."

Mack and I exchanged a look. Heloise. We might know what she was doing, but the rest of the staff at the clinic didn't have a clue. That aspect of the investigation was still under tight wraps, as we wanted to get our ducks in neat little rows before making more arrests. Every damn *I* had to be dotted, and every *T* crossed before we could hand things over to the district attorney, where things would be handled by the prosecutors. Sure, they would be in contact with us throughout, and we would be called to testify when the case went to court, but officially, we considered the case closed once the DA had it. And our present DA was a stickler. She did *not* want one criminal getting off on a technicality or due to sloppy police procedure. We didn't either, but Monique Mason was a whole new level of detail-oriented. Given that we were working numerous cases at the same time—and were fried like eggs from being overworked on the daily—we had to double down on ensuring no mistakes were made on our end.

"You work closely with Heloise?" I asked.

I sensed Mack stiffening next to me. Was this kid connected to her? Was he part of this scheme? Had he crossed a line?

"God no, she kinda scares me a little, and she's super territorial over billing… I mostly avoid her."

"Please, go on," Mack said as I lingered in the corner, arms crossed, belly rumbling softly. Too much coffee and no food. The story of my life.

"So yeah, I'm gathering up the billings for Medicare to send to Heloise when I hear something at the front door. I thought it was maybe Dilbert, so I got up to go let him in."

Mack shot me a questioning look. I shook my head. That was a name that I had not heard in our previous discussions with the clinic staff.

"Dilbert?" Mack asked.

Lazlo blushed. "He's an alley cat that I feed every day. Heloise says she's allergic and isn't really keen on the cat hanging around, so I do it on the sly. He's a really nice cat. He digs on the front or back door, then I take him whatever kind of cat food I buy at the dollar store. It stinks really bad, the tuna food, but Dilbert loves it."

"Cats are cool," Mack said with a patient smile. "So, the sound at the door. Was it the cat?"

"No, it was some dude trying to jimmy the lock open. I yelled at him to stop. That was when he pulled out the gun and fired through the glass. The alarm went off, and he had like this second of not knowing what to do, so he froze, and that was when I saw his face. When our eyes locked, he freaked out and shot like a dozen times." There had been only three shots fired through the glass, but I was sure it seemed like hundreds to poor Lazlo. "One of them hit me as I was trying to run back to the reception desk. It really hurt."

The door to his cubby hole of a room opened, and the doctor entered. "My patient needs to rest. Tie this up."

This time, the man in white stayed in the room. Our time was over, it seemed.

"You said you recognized the man? Can you give us more information?" Mack asked as I reached for my phone.

"Yeah, he had a scar in the shape of a Z, you know, like Zorro." Mack and I both nodded. "I remembered seeing him waiting outside the clinic a few weeks ago. He was there with his baby mama. Some tiny thing with a newborn, her name is Karen Snipes. Like Wesley Snipes. You can find her file at the clinic. I don't know his name, but I bet she does, since she and her baby got into his car after the appointment."

"Thank you for this information. We'll be in touch. I hope you recover quickly," Mack said as I nodded along.

"Do you guys know what's going on?" Lazlo asked. We did, but we weren't at liberty to say a thing yet. So, we did what all cops do when they really want to help ease a victim's mind but can't.

"We're working on things and hope to have news for you soon. Thank you, Doctor."

Mack eased out of the room. I followed, and we were hustling ass to get to Mack's car. We'd have to find Karen Snipes' records back at the clinic. That was the easy part, or, I should say, the least dangerous part. All we had to do was tell the manager of the clinic that the files possibly held information vital to apprehending a suspect in a crime. HIPAA rules gave us the right to grab medical records without a warrant in order to identify a suspect, witness, fugitive, or missing person. And I was sure that Joe would give that file over with all haste, as his clinic would be teetering on the brink of financial ruin if we didn't get this mess cleaned up fast.

I glared at the banana-yellow Honda as we moved toward it. I should have insisted we take my car, but I'd caved when I met Mack at his place. We folded ourselves into the car and off we went to the Haven of Hope clinic. Mack was driving, and I was on the phone, trying to contact anyone to unlock the clinic so we could get into Joe's files. Turned out Joe was out of hospital, and the man finally answered and was more than agreeable to give us what we needed. Again, I knew Joe was stressed to the max and filled with questions, but he'd have to wait a little longer. All would be revealed in due time.

I wished I could contact Oliver to fill him in. Instead of doing something that would be a major no-no, I sent him a fast text saying that I was flexing my *Hill Street Blues* vibes. That got me a reply with a meme of Sergeant

Esterhaus and his famous, "Hey, let's be careful out there" line.

I promised I'd be, then added an *X* because I guess I was doing that now. If anyone had told me I'd be signing off on texts with kisses two months ago, I'd have laughed in their face.

THE CLINIC WAS IN DISARRAY, YET AGAIN, WHEN MACK and I met a pale and shaky Joe outside.

"Should you be back so soon?" I asked.

Joe shrugged, then winced. "I'll go stir-crazy at home," he said, and I wasn't going to argue with that.

The front door had been sealed with plywood, the blood stains in the reception area were being mopped up as we spoke, and a scraggly little yellow cat was napping on the desk where Lazlo should've been seated.

"File room is back here," Joe told us, leading us past the remaining staff who were working madly to get things set to rights. There were people out there who needed this place badly. "I'm surprised any of them even showed up to work. I wouldn't blame anyone for quitting, given how dangerous this clinic has become."

"They're dedicated to serving, just like you," I said softly and got a funny look from Joe, who still didn't seem as if he should be scrubbing blood from tiles.

"Seems to be a thing with some of us, huh?" He stopped outside a small office, opened the door, and waved at walls of files. "We keep paper files, as well as storing them on the computer. Call me old-fashioned, but I like to know I have paper in hand when Skynet takes over the world."

"Smart man," Mack said, as he, too, disliked our reliance on technology.

"Anything you can tell me that I can pass along to my staff?" Joe asked.

We fed him some of the standard lines, but were able to add that Lazlo would be discharged as soon as his brother arrived from Oregon. That news cheered Joe up, our lack of information for him did not, and I was sorry for that.

Once inside the file room, we dug out Karen Snipes' folder. The girl was just twenty and had given birth a month ago. Her file, which went back about four years, was filled with questionable injuries that had strongly prompted the attending physician to suspect domestic abuse. Karen fell down stairs a lot. Karen tripped into open cupboards a lot. Karen lived with a man named Philip Miscotti, aged thirty-two, who was recorded as the father of her newborn baby girl, Poppy. Mack placed the call to run Miscotti through the database, while I read over the long list of broken bones and black eyes Karen had presented with over the past two years.

Good old Phil's criminal background report was a cornucopia of run-ins with the law since he was fourteen. Phil liked to rob people, beat up people, and terrorize people. Phil also had been in prison twice on two different charges of possession of illegal prescription medications with the intent to sell. Both times, our buddy Ivan Baladin's lawyer had bailed him out and acted as his counsel. Coincidence? Not likely. Smirking at the link between these two scum balls, I relayed what Berke had found out online for us, then set a few things into motion as Mack and I left the clinic to go visit Karen Snipes.

"So what? Ivan sends this Phil guy to get whatever he was after when he sent in that Periapsis asshole?"

"Maybe so."

"For passwords."

"Yep."

"He's a fucking idiot."

I set up some backup for when we went to visit Ms. Snipes and her boyfriend—who was assumed to be living with her—as well as tracking down a judge willing to cough up a warrant. I managed to get an unmarked with fellow detectives, as well as a lone marked that would show up at the address as soon as we had it. The warrant didn't arrive for two hours, which gave Mack and me time to stop and buy some hot dogs and devour them. We lingered around the public housing apartments on Sunset Boulevard, cramped and hot inside Mack's Honda, until the warrant came down. Then, we met with our backups, had a short talk about how this was hopefully going to go down, and went to knock on Karen's door on the fourth floor of the massive low-income housing complex. Mack and I alone, with our fellow police officers on standby.

Berke and Mason were in the lobby, loitering about while trying not to look conspicuous, while our newest additions were parked out front in unmarked cars.

Mack knocked on the door of 487, which set off a baby's wail. A male voice inside bellowed. The baby cried louder. Mack gave me a sideways glance. I stood quietly, listening, wary. Any time you paid a known violent felon a friendly visit, things could get screwed up in a heartbeat.

Karen opened the door. She was a tiny thing, tired brown eyes, long brown hair knotted into a bun atop her head. Her bottom lip was discolored and puffy.

"Please help me, officers? He's going to hurt Poppy soon."

Did we really look that much like cops? Guess so…

Mack began to reply. Phil, in all his Zorro scar-faced glory, charged at the door and grabbed Karen by the hair, his eyes wild and glazed. The baby inside the tiny apartment wailed more loudly as Phil slammed Karen's face into the door jamb. She went slack. Phil threw her at Mack, then dove at me. He wasn't a large man, not nearly as tall as me, but he had some meat on his bones. We stumbled back into a door, our bulk and force busting the flimsy lock.

I felt the impact of something into my side. A knife probably, thankfully, blocked by the Kevlar vest I'd pulled on before our little social visit.

"Philip Miscotti, you're under arrest for assaulting an officer, as well as under the suspicion of attempted murder of Lazlo Richter," I shouted at Phil in English, then in Spanish. "You have the right to—"

"Fuck you, pig!" he snarled, his pupils blown, clearly on something. Then, the fucker tried to bite me on the cheek. I grabbed his head and pushed back.

"Remain silent. Anything you say can and will be used against you in a court of law. Fuckhead, stop trying to bite me!"

He shook his head like a mad dog as he tried to chomp down on my forearms now. "I eat pork!" Phil growled.

"You have the right to an attorney. If you cannot afford one, one will be provided to you. If you decide to answer questions now without an attorney present—stop trying to bite me!"

"Pork, pork, pork! Yummy raw pork!" His jaws snapped together rapidly.

"Without an attorney present, you will still have the right to stop answering—goddamn it—at any time until you talk to an attorney. Do you understand these rights as I have read them to you? Ow, motherfucker, stop trying to bite me!"

His teeth found purchase on my thumb. I yelped.

An older woman in a checkered dress appeared out of nowhere, shouted at Phil in rapid-fire Spanish, then cracked him over the head with a steel frying pan. Phil collapsed on top of me in a heap, his head bleeding and coated with what looked to be fried ground beef, avocado, rice, green and red peppers, and pinto beans. The rather delicious-smelling concoction tumbled down over me as well.

"He is a shit-faced woman beater," the woman announced in Spanish while I shoved Phil off me, then sat up, pinto beans rolling to my lap.

Footsteps thundered down the hallway as I sat there flicking beans off my pants while my savior informed me of every offense Phil had ever visited upon her. Guess he got his just desserts.

I suspected poor Karen would agree.

Chapter Nineteen

Oliver

IN THE KITCHEN, THE ONLY SOUND WAS THE QUIET HUM OF the refrigerator and my own steady breathing. It had been two days since I'd last seen Jackson, and the sparse messages that passed between us did little to fill the silence left in his absence. The demands of his badge consumed his time—that much was clear.

Today, I'd made my way to the clinic, slipping in through the back to avoid any unnecessary attention. Seeing Lazlo back at work, his smile a little less bright, but just as determined, had been a relief. And Joe, although still visibly shaken, was holding up. I knew there was more to the story, details that Jackson held, but for now, I was thankful that the good guys hadn't lost. Not this time.

Jamie had turned in for the night after our customary check on the girls, who were sound asleep. Tomorrow promised a rare rest day for the team before the flight to New York in the afternoon—a trip that made me nervous, anxious, but also so damn excited.

I was just about to lock up when the gate buzzer cut

through the stillness of the night. Moving to the intercom, I pressed the button, and the screen flickered to life, revealing Jackson on the other side. My heart skipped a beat at the sight of him.

"Jackson?" I said, my voice betraying my surprise.

"Yeah, it's me. Can I come in?" His voice was the same, steady and sure, but I heard an undercurrent of something I couldn't quite place.

I opened the gate for him, then waited at the front door, anticipation coiling tight in my stomach. What brought him here so late without warning? Was it because he was as desperate to see me as I was him? His footsteps on the gravel announced his arrival, and then, he stepped into the light of the porch, and I was down the few steps in an instant, yanking him into a hug and breathing in the scent of him as he buried himself in my neck. We stood there for the longest time, and when he pulled back, he rested his forehead on mine.

"You're a sight for sore eyes," he whispered.

"I missed you."

"Not as much as I missed you," he deadpanned.

"Let's go inside, okay?"

He nodded, though it didn't quite reach his eyes. "Yeah, just… it's been a long couple of days. I was going to wait to get a shower, or… but I just needed to see you."

"Well, you've seen me," I replied, a half-smile forming on my lips, as I guided him into the hall and shut the door. He leaned against the wall.

"When you're not with me, it hurts," he blurted, and crossed his arms over his chest. "I'm obsessed."

I blinked at him, not sure how to handle that statement

—unless of course I told him the truth that I was obsessed right back. "You want coffee or something?"

Jackson's lips twitched in response, a shadow of his usual smirk, and his gaze locked onto mine. I felt that electric charge, that pull between us, that hadn't diminished one bit in the time he'd been absent. He reached out a hand to me, and I took it, closing the distance between us, reading the quiet plea written across his face for a kiss. The world outside faded into nothingness as I reached up to cup the back of his neck, drawing him closer. Our lips met, and it was as if we'd never been apart. His touch was at my waist, pulling me in until there was no space left between us, until everything was about the here and now.

"Missed you so much," he murmured, then slumped a little.

I held him up. "Missed you too."

"I think I'm falling in love with you," he whispered.

"Me too."

I tugged him to the stairs, and we climbed, and he leaned on me for support. I didn't think he was hurt, just plain old exhausted, and I guided him past the girls' rooms, where we met Jamie as he emerged from the family bathroom.

"Jackson," he acknowledged.

"Mmmm," Jackson said and yawned. I'm not sure he was entirely with us by then.

"Your boyfriend needs to sleep," Jamie observed. He had a point.

"Shower first," Jackson nearly whimpered, and Jamie winked as I tugged Jackson into my room, shut the door, stripped him and me, then took him into the shower. There was nothing sexual about this—he needed to be clean, he needed sleep, and I wanted to look after him. I dried him off with fluffy towels, rummaged for a clean pair of pajamas so he didn't end up walking naked around my house, then tucked him into bed. He pulled me down next to him, and after some wriggling, he turned to me and buried his face in my neck again.

"Are you okay?" I whispered and pressed a kiss to his damp hair.

"Hmmm."

"Do I need to set the alarm for you?"

"Nah… day off…" He yawned and buried deeper.

"Sleep then," I ordered.

"Love you," he said, and my heart leaped.

"Love you, back," I whispered.

He mumbled something, and sighed. "Yeah, pork…"

"What?"

But all I got was soft breathing and the occasional snuffle.

And it was perfect.

———

THE CHILL OF THE NEW YORK NIGHTHAWKS ICE WAS A welcome shock to my system as I waited in the tunnel, ready to step out and face my old team. I'd left Jackson at home playing Uno with Jamie and the girls. He'd actually slept through to eleven, and given I had to leave about then, we'd done little more than kiss, but he looked better, rested.

His goodbye kiss was still warm on my lips, even now. Jamie had promised to monitor him, and the girls loved having him there. Jackson kind of fit, and it was good.

He hadn't repeated his declaration of love, but then, neither had I.

Until I was at the arena, and he was hip deep in games with the girls.

Jackson: I love you

Oli: I love you back

Jackson: Good luck out there, Superman

Luck wasn't what we needed against New York tonight. They were coming off a seven-game winning streak, their momentum a force to be reckoned with. We needed a miracle.

"We can do this," Charles summed up at the end of a rousing speech in the locker room, and there was no space for any of us to disagree. If a team went into a game thinking of loss, then it was almost a self-fulfilling prophecy. This was only our first game on this east coast stand; we were also playing the Rebels, the Railers, and Carolina all in their barns. It was intense, and I already missed the girls like a limb.

And Jackson.

"You okay?" Ash asked from my side, as the jumbotron showcased a montage of my years with New York—the saves, the assists, the body checks. The crowd roared for me, a sound that was familiar, but weird given I wasn't a Nighthawk anymore. A twinge of nostalgia mixed with adrenaline, but I tapped Ash's calf.

"I'm good."

"Get out there then. Take a bow!" Ash nearly shoved me through the gate to do a solo lap before the game started. As I took to the ice, acknowledging the cheers with a raised stick, I felt a surge of pride in the city, my old team, and in myself. These were my roots, but I was here to show the fans how much I'd grown. And then, with the roar still echoing in my ears, it was game on.

The puck dropped and instinct took over. We played hard, each of us knowing that against a team of New York's caliber, there was no room for error. Every pass, every shot, every check was deliberate, intense.

I skated with a ferocity I reserved for games like this. The Nighthawks guys were strong, but we had our own strengths. We were the Storm, and tonight, we would show them that we could be just as formidable.

"Watch Callahan," Coach warned. "He's all over Charles."

"On it, Coach," Ash and I choroused.

We were in sync, a defensive duo that had grown to anticipate each other's moves on the ice. Our skates carved deep grooves as we went over the boards and circled our zone, eyes on the Nighthawks forwards, weaving our way. They came at us like a well-oiled machine, their winning streak giving them a ton of confidence.

One of their wingers broke away, puck on his stick, charging toward our goal with the weight of the team behind him. I glanced at Ash, a silent signal passing between us. We tightened our formation, a wall of determination.

As the winger drew back his stick for a shot, I stepped forward. The timing had to be perfect. Too soon, and he'd sidestep me. Too late and the puck would be past our goalie before we could blink. I thrust my stick out, tapping the puck enough to throw off his shot. It skidded away toward the boards, the threat momentarily cleared.

But the Nighthawks were relentless. Another forward snatched up the loose puck, sending it back to their point man. The shot came in hard and fast, a blur headed for the top shelf where grandma hides the cookies, but Ash was there, body first into the line of fire. The puck ricocheted off his pads with a thud, and suddenly, we were turning defense into offense.

I scooped up the puck, adrenaline fueling my charge up the ice. Craig Beaulieu did his whole pirouette-to-avoid-getting-hit thing up against the boards, taking the focus away from Charles and gathering interest from the Nighthawks defense—he used his childhood skills as a figure skater to dazzle even the best defenseman. I know— I'd been on the other side of his antics too many times to mention. Charles was already breaking away, his stick raised in anticipation. I feinted a pass to the left, drawing a defender to me, before sliding the puck across to Charles with a crisp tap.

Our captain's speed was a blur, his focus absolute. He took the puck in stride, barely breaking form as he approached the Nighthawks' netminder. With a deke that sent the goalie sprawling the wrong way, Charles flicked the puck into the gaping net, the sound of it hitting the back music to our ears.

The arena erupted, the fans in purple screaming as the red light glared. Charles threw his head back, the relief and triumph clear on his face as we swarmed him, our cheers almost as loud as the crowd's.

"Goal!" Ash shouted over the din, his glove slapping my shoulder.

"Fuck yes!" I agreed, the grin on my face matching his. This was teamwork, this was the Storm, and we were more than holding our own against the Nighthawks. We were defining ourselves, one goal at a time.

I was fitting in. I was doing things right.

As the game went on, the score see-sawed. They were good, but somehow, we were matching them, play for play, and when the final buzzer sounded, it was our sticks raised in victory. We had pulled off the impossible, defeating a giant. And I knew, as the crowd's roar filled the arena, that we hadn't just needed a miracle—we *were* the miracle.

WE LANDED BACK AT VAN NUYS AFTER EIGHT GRUELING days, two wins, two losses, and the mood in the Storm jet was a mix of exhaustion and relief.

The engines wound down on the Storm's private jet, and boy, was I glad to be back in LA.

Coach stood at the front of the cabin as the jet taxied to our hangar, his gaze passing over each of us. "Take tomorrow off," he said, his voice cutting through the murmur of tired conversations. "Rest up, spend time with your families, and forget about hockey for a day. I want you back in the barn on Tuesday, bright and early, ready to work."

A collective sigh rippled through the team, a mixture of relief and the remnants of fatigue. We had given it our all, every check, every shot, every save, but we were all so damn tired.

I nodded along with my teammates, already thinking of a quiet day ahead. No rink, no gear, just time to recharge and to think about… well, about everything. The thought of Jamie and the girls at the house awaiting me put a spring in my step, and I knew Jackson was coming over as well—he'd messaged he'd be there. As the cabin doors opened, we shuffled out, each man lost in his thoughts. Some had cars waiting, but I was getting a ride with Ash and his girlfriend, and didn't even register that I had someone there until Scarlett and Daisy threw themselves at me.

"Daddy!" Daisy yelled up at me, and I went to a crouch to gather them close and hug them hard. They smelled of cookies and home, and I'd missed them so much. Jamie stood back from them, grinning, but it was the man next to him who caught my eye.

Jackson was here.

Waiting for me to get home.

Charles stopped to chat with Jackson. They exchanged fist bumps and bro-hugs, and I went back to focusing on my girls. They peppered my face with kisses, talking over each other.

"… then we did pancakes, and we had cream and strawberries, and it was yum—"

"… Jackson ate so many, and Uncle Jamie laughed…"

"… we made more, and they'll be cold, but you can have them…"

"… I dropped Annie-bear in the pond…"

"… We iced cupcakes…"

"… she got all wet, but Jackson fixed it for me…"

"… and then Jamie made scones, and we have more cream and jelly, and that was nom as well…"

I scooped both my girls up—Scarlett was maybe getting too big at seven to want her daddy carrying her, but I needed this right now, and she wrapped her hands around me and kissed me again.

They were everything.

Jackson pulled me and the girls into a hug, stealing the quickest of kisses. "You came," I murmured.

"I wanted to welcome the man I love home," he deadpanned. "Live with it."

And I realized at that moment, I'd do more than live with it. I'd take him and hold him close and never let him go.

Epilogue

Jackson

IT WAS FUNNY, IN THAT NOT-FUNNY WAY, HOW MUCH A person's life could change in such a short amount of time.

Last year, as the weather started to cool a little—Los Angeles didn't get super cold, as it's no Vermont, but the temps did dip a bit in fall—I'd been working nonstop. Eager to fill the emptiness in my life with nicotine, whiskey, and long days chasing down bad guys. I still worked too hard, but now I took time off to enjoy things. Like a fast day trip to Big Bear with Oliver, the girls, Jamie aka Nanny Belvedere, Bryce, and Leo to see some fall colors.

I did things like pick apples, carve pumpkins, make paper plate turkeys, and read bedtime stories about princesses and dragons. Bryce liked to tease that the feral cat of the family had finally found someone to domesticate him. Jamie commented that, perhaps, someone should dock my ear in case I reverted to my feral state, so no one would try to neuter me again.

Oliver would chide his friend, but I could handle the Brit's teasing. A lot of what he was saying was true. I *was* like an alley cat in many regards. I needed love and affection, but I was too hissy to accept it until someone with patience had lovingly taken the time to work past my defenses. Was I neutered? Yeah, maybe. I had no drive to sleep around any more. My nights were spent curled up on the sofa with a full belly and Oliver stroking my hair. Why would I venture out into the mean streets when I had it so good here? Jamie's gag gift of a feather dangler cat toy might have gotten my fur up a bit, but I smiled sweetly, and then, a week later, left a neatly folded '*The British Blew a Thirteen-Colony Lead'* T-shirt on his bed.

It was typical family shit, and I loved it. It was what I had needed. My sister had been right all along, something she took great joy in pointing out every damn time we spoke. Older sisters could be so superior.

Four weeks had passed since we had officially turned the money laundering case over to the district attorney. Mack and I were still overworked and underpaid, as most civil servants were, but we now had four pairs of detectives in our division, so we could at least pause to breathe. The Feds had been interested in some of our findings in the Baladin case, which had led to them joining with us on a concurrent jurisdiction case involving Ivan's family. All that malarkey about rivalries between local and state with the FBI is just Hollywood drama. For the most part, law enforcement is grateful for any aid in taking down the nogoodniks. The face-eating druggie who'd shot Lazlo had sobered up and turned evidence on Baladin, said he'd been threatened to break in and find passwords. He admitted that he had no fucking clue what he'd been looking for, and Baladin had really been clutching at straws.

I still felt sick at the feel of his teeth in my skin.

Freaky zombie shit gave me nightmares.

So that was one of six ongoing cases that Mack and I were working on, with trips to court added in whenever we were needed. My time at home had become precious to me, and I guarded it like that feral cat Jamie teased me about being.

"You look tired," Oliver said, busting into my mental meander. "We can go home soon," he added.

"I'm good. We need to celebrate," I replied, taking a sip of my punch, then moving a step to the side to slide my arm around his waist.

The front lobby of the Haven of Hope was packed with friends and supporters for a re-re-reopening party. The LA Storm had turned out in force to support the cause—donations flowing in, I was sure—as had several of my fellow cops. Mack and Elena were here talking to Lazlo, who was cuddling Dilbert, the alley cat. Joe was chatting it up with my ex-brother-in-law, Bryce, and his man, Mike, while Leo and Oliver's girls were sitting in the newly finished playroom eating cookies, sipping pink punch, and coloring in pages on how to avoid catching colds. "This is a big night."

"Still, you need to slow down," he said as I reached over to pluck a cookie from a tray being carried to the buffet table by one of the catering staff. "And eat better."

I popped the cookie in and chewed. Oliver was such a

stickler for proper nutrition that we sometimes had little spats over my less than stellar eating habits.

"Hey, I've given up smoking and booze. I need one vice," I parried, tossing the same line I always used when he would criticize my junk food adoration. He rolled his eyes, kissed me tenderly, and then was pulled into a conversation with his defensive partner. I broke off a moment later to follow the cookie tray to one of the long buffet tables. "Come to Papa," I whispered, filling a cloth napkin with sugary treats.

"Your boyfriend is giving you dark looks," Bryce said softly as he came up beside me.

"Block his view. I need the rush to get me through tonight," I told him.

"Oh no, I'm not being an accessory to your cookie crimes," Bryce snickered, but still stepped into place to shield me from my lover. "You owe me for this."

"Yeah, yeah, whatever you want, just stand there and let me gorge," I said around a mouthful of white raspberry roll-up cookies.

"We're short on volunteers this weekend at the garden," he informed me. I knew just where this was going. "If you could come by and help us set up for our annual biggest pumpkin contest, I would really appreciate it."

"Bryce, seriously?" He took a step back, clearing the line of sight between Oliver and me. "Shit, okay, fine. I'll come help tote pumpkins. Now get back to where you were."

"Good. Leo has to fly back home the following day, but we were hoping to do the contest and then, possibly, drive out to Idyllwild to camp overnight. There's supposed to be a meteor shower that night, and he's really been getting into stars and space."

"Sounds nice."

"Would you like to come? It'll only be us three, but we have room in the tent for a fourth."

"Nah, thanks, I'm planning on vegging this weekend. Oliver's playing at home for a nice stretch, so I want to spend whatever time I can with him and the girls. What?"

He patted my biceps. "Nothing, I'm just very happy for you. I was worried you were becoming a little too dependent on the bottle there for a bit, but falling in love has worked wonders for you. Now, if Oliver could get you to change your ties more often."

I glanced down. Well shit. Not only was there mustard from the hot dog I'd inhaled for lunch while Mack and I had been interviewing witnesses to a drive-by shooting being pinned on the Yellow Boys, but there was also raspberry jam. The Yellow Boys, an up-and-coming street gang that was taking over territory like a tsunami, were on our radar for the usual drugs and weapons peddling, as well as rumors of them dabbling in the bribery of local district judges. They were proud as fuck about their affiliations and wore bright yellow bandanas.

"I did remind him to change his tie before he left the precinct," Oliver said, sliding into the conversation.

Seeing that there was no way to hide the napkin overflowing with cookies, I merely shoved an oatmeal raisin into my mouth.

"Well, even a miracle worker like you runs into a

stumbling block," Bryce teased, gave Oliver a wink, and left me alone to face the music.

"Okay, before you start, my sugar was incredibly low this evening," I explained, cradling my stash of carbs and raspberry filling to my chest.

"You're pulling a low sugar line on a type one diabetic?" he asked incredulously.

"Yeah. No. But I'm taking some home for Jamie."

His flat look told me he wasn't buying that for a second. "I hope you have enough stamina after your incoming sugar crash to play a grown-up game with me after the girls go to bed."

Oh. Oh, a grown-up game. That sounded promising. I dumped the cookies back onto the tray and got a kiss from my man. He wet his lips to draw in the cookie crumbs left behind from our smooch. My weary body responded as it always did when he did that. Blood flowed south.

"So, yeah, is it time to go yet?" I asked, as visions of naughtiness danced in my head.

"SO THAT X IN PIXEL IS ON A TRIPLE WORD SCORE square," Oliver gloated as we sat at his kitchen table at midnight, playing Scrabble.

"Just to reiterate, this is not at all what I had envisioned when you said adult games," I informed him, and got a sly smile.

"You're just mad that you're losing." He tallied up his score, then took a sip of hot chocolate. Smug. Smugness oozed off the man. It was incredibly sexy, I had to admit.

"I'm not mad. My dick is disappointed," I clarified as I studied my tiles.

"Daisy isn't sleeping well since she saw that movie the other night," he replied with a pointed look at me.

"In my defense, yet again, when I saw it was a movie about a princess and a dragon, I had no idea that the dragon was in the habit of feasting on innocent princesses, instead of giving them fun sky rides through the clouds."

"They have a thing called a rating system," Oliver reminded me, yet again. I huffed and placed an *E* on top of his *X*, then stared at him right in his beautiful dark eyes.

"There, ex. If I had anything other than vowels, I would spell out extraordinarily sad penis to claim victory right here and now."

He stared at my *E* with suspicion. "Is that a valid word?"

"Of course. Look it up."

He did because of course he did. The man took Scrabble very seriously. The last time we'd played with Jamie, he'd argued up and down that Jamie's use of bellend was not a valid Scrabble word. Jamie said it was in the British Dictionary and that Americans knew nothing. Turned out, Oliver was right, and Jamie had to remove his word and lose all the points. Things got rabid in the Cowan house on Scrabble night, let me tell you.

"Okay, that's acceptable," Oliver said after checking his phone. "It's a good job I love you," he added.

I gloated for a moment, then sat back to enjoy his pretty face. I could stare at this man forever and never tire of it. He was stunning. So masculine it robbed me of breath sometimes. His gaze lifted to meet mine, and he smiled.

"This is nice, isn't it?" He said.

It was. Very nice. The house was quiet, the room still carrying the finest scent of garlic from the garlic knots we'd had with our rigatoni. The girls loved sewer pipes, as they called them. Even with my new dedication to taking more time to be here, Oliver and I shared precious few nights like this. His hockey schedule was insane. How they maintained an eighty-game pace, I had no clue. Hockey players were a different breed.

"Yeah, it's really nice," I had to admit as the tiniest sound floated to us.

An itty-bitty squeak like that of a yawning field mouse. I turned to look over my shoulder to see Daisy in the doorway, her nightgown wrinkled, her hair knotted, and her nose red.

"Hey, you," I called. She ran barefoot over the tiles to me, surprising me greatly, as she usually wanted her daddy when she had bad dreams. I lifted her from the floor. The girl was light as pixie dust. I settled her on my lap.

"Was it that mean dragon again?"

She nodded, sniffled, and let her head rest on my chest. I glanced at Oliver, who was watching us with the most besotted expression I had ever seen.

"What's you playing?" Daisy asked, her thumb resting on her lower lip, something that she tended to do when she was upset or stressed. Self-soothing, Oliver called it.

"Scrabble," I answered, shifting her bony backside to the left. She clung like a burdock, the sweet scent of peach shampoo wafting off her hair.

"Can I play?"

I looked at Oliver questioningly.

"Maybe for a little, then you have to go back to bed. You have school in the morning, I have morning skate, and Jackson has to go to work," Oliver explained patiently.

"Stopping the bad men," Daisy whispered, then gave my scruffy cheek a pat.

"Yep, stopping the bad men," Oliver replied before clearing the board to start a new game.

Daisy sat up straighter as we arranged tiles on the wooden stands.

"What's you drinking? Coffee?" she enquired, fingering her tiles thoughtfully.

"Jackson is, I'm having cocoa. Would you like some warm milk?" Oliver asked and got a nod.

He rose to warm some milk, as Daisy and I plotted our moves in top secret tones.

"Daddy, Jackson and me is going to make words you can't beat. I know how to spell so good!"

Oliver chortled, placed a mug in front of his daughter, and was about to reply when his gaze flew to the doorway. I craned my head. There was Scarlett, all sleep-rumpled and confused, her tiny toes bared.

"Is someone sick?" Scarlett asked. Ever the worrier.

"Nope, your sister had a bad dream," I told her. "Now, we're playing Scrabble to help her get sleepy because it's the most boring game ever in the history of games."

Scarlett giggled, then grew serious. "Can I play and have some warm milk, please?"

Her father sighed before giving her the briefest of

nods. "One game, one mug of milk, and then both of you are going back to bed."

"Daisy can sleep with me if she's still scared," Scarlett offered graciously before taking her seat and setting up her own stand with tiles. "Are you two playing as a team?"

"Maybe, but don't worry, Daisy knows way more words than I do," I told Scarlett while Oliver puttered about making everyone warm milk. I gave my mug a sour look.

"Don't make a bad face. Daddy puts vanilla in it."

"Oh okay, vanilla makes everything better," I said.

Oliver sat down across from me. The girls were given the nod to go first, and Daisy spelled out *DOG* for our first word. We high-fived. Scarlett was pondering her move when I felt a big, warm, sock-covered foot find mine under the table. My gaze met Oliver's. Love and contentment filled me. I wasn't sure how one big dude, plus two little girls, could have added up to everything I never knew I needed, but they did.

"Oh, I have this word," Scarlett announced as she hurried to place an *L*, a *V*, and an *E* using the *O* in Daisy's *DOG* to make the word *LOVE*.

I guess love was just as easy to spell out as it was to fall into.

THE END

Free Story

The case is closed, the vows are half-written, and the backyard is drowning in pink—but the groom is nowhere to be found.

Set after *Spiral*, this short story brings you one last dose of chaos, love, and laughter from the LA Storm crew —because not even a wedding goes smoothly when Jackson and Oli are involved.

https://geni.us/lasoulmates

What's next for LA Storm?

Spiral (LA Storm book 4)

Where the worlds of academia and sports collide, a doctor of math and a dyslexic hockey star solve the equation for love.

In the middle of game-changing research on the never-ending Fibonacci spiral, Dr. Jameson Hennessey hits the reset button on his life. Post-breakup, he heads to the other side of the country to crash with his best friend, doubling as a part-time nanny and working on his research every spare moment. When Jamie finds out that a hated rival, the same ex he's just left, is working on his ideas, he has to up his game and looks to the sports for inspiration, in particular Craig, winger, former figure skater, and the sexiest man he's ever laid eyes on. Initially, Jamie's all about the math, wanting Craig's help to crack the code on predicting sports moves with the Fibonacci sequence. At first, their worlds collide—Jamie buttoned-up and focused, Craig prickly and defensive—but as they team up, something unexpected happens. Amidst late-night study sessions and ice rink chill-outs, Jamie finds that maybe there's a formula for love, and Craig might just be the answer he wasn't even looking for.

Craig Beaulieu has made it to the pros through pure grit and determination. As a child, his dyslexia made his hours spent in the classroom difficult. Thankfully, he had the ice to retreat to when things at school got too intense. His skill on skates led him first into figure skating as a pairs partner to his twin sister and then to ice hockey, where he worked twice as hard as the other guys to make sense of all those X's and O's. With the help of an understanding high school coach, Craig was able to make the collegiate hockey team where he was picked up by the Storm for his speed, grace, and ability to light the lamp. Life is rolling along smoothly, if not a little solitary, when he meets Jamie at a team party. He's instantly attracted to the handsome Brit and wholly unprepared to be asked to take part in some sort of mathematical study about sports movement. Drawn to Jamie, but leery of looking out-of-place with the brightest minds in academia, he agrees to take part in the study just to gawk at the handsome professor. Things don't start well at all, but Craig falls hard and fast despite all his fancy moves both on and off the ice.

Hockey Series' from RJ Scott & V.L. Locey

Harrisburg Railers

Owatonna U Hockey

Arizona Raptors

Boston Rebels

LA Storm

Chesterford Coyotes - Young Adult

Railers Legacy

Rochester Copperheads (AHL, coming soon)

Oxford Knights (coming 2027)

Railers Legacy

Speed (Railers Legacy 1)

Hard ice. Fast cars. Fierce love.

And a race against fate.

Hockey is as natural as breathing for Noah. Growing up with two
famous hockey stars as his dads, Noah has always aspired to join
the Railers to continue the Lyamin-Gunnarsson legacy. With his
degree done, it's time to live that dream, and the first step is
being drafted by the team his hall-of-fame dad played for. The
second step is to pull on that dusky blue-gray sweater and make
his fathers proud. His rookie year is bound to be a season of
incredible highs and lows, but one of the biggest highlights is
meeting Brody Vance at a fundraiser. Brody is the living epitome

of a bad boy hiding his pain behind a devil-may-care attitude. As Noah struggles to keep one eye on the puck and not on Brody, it's only a matter of time before both loves collide in a chaotic splash of media attention.

Bad boy racing driver Brody has spent his life chasing speed and glory and is only points away from his first world championship when a devastating crash ends his season. Determined to make a triumphant comeback, Brody is blindsided by a diagnosis that forces him off the track for good. With his world flipped upside down and family and fans questioning why he left, Brody hides his pain by pushing the limits and refusing to let anyone see the cracks. But after a chance meeting with a sweet, sexy hockey player turns into an unforgettable one-night stand, fate keeps putting Noah in his path. With his heart on the line and his body racing against time, Brody must decide if he's willing to risk it all for love—or if he'll let fear and pride leave him in the dust.

Speed is a steamy M/M romance with a hockey rookie living his family legacy, a bad-boy racing driver with secrets, media attention that would break even the strongest of men, an unforgettable one-night stand, a love that means risking it all, and a hard-won happily ever after.

Railers Legacy

1. *Speed*
2. *Blitz*
3. *Powder*
4. *Fly*

Harrisburg Railers

When hockey wunderkind Tennant Rowe meets his new coach, he knows he's in trouble. Jared Madsen is nine years older than Tennant, impossibly attractive, and — worst of all — his brother's off-limits best friend. Is their chemistry worth the risk?

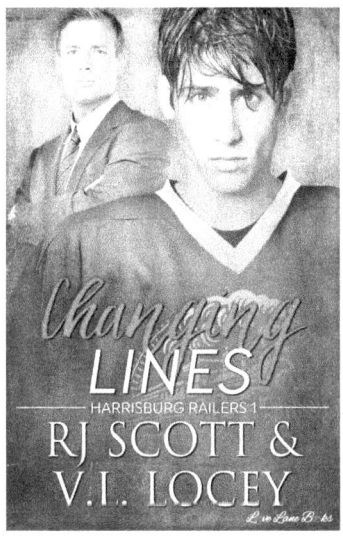

Changing Lines (Railers 1)

Can Tennant show Jared that age is just a number, and that love is all that matters?

The Rowe Brothers are famous hockey hotshots, but as the youngest of the trio, Tennant has always had to play against his brothers' reputations. To get out of their shadows, and against their advice, he accepts a trade to the Harrisburg Railers, where he runs into Jared Madsen. Mads is an old family friend and his brother's one-time teammate. Mads is Tennant's new coach. And Mads is the sexiest thing he's ever laid eyes on.

Jared Madsen's hockey career was cut short by a fault in his heart, but coaching keeps him close to the game. When Ten is traded to the team, his carefully organized world is thrown into chaos. Nine years his junior and his best friend's brother, he knows Ten is strictly off-limits, but as soon as he sees Ten's moves, on and off the ice, he knows that his heart could get him into trouble again.

Harrisburg Railers (Hockey Romance)

1. Changing Lines
2. First Season
3. Deep Edge
4. Poke Check
5. Last Defense
6. Goal Line
7. Neutral Zone
8. Hat Trick
9. Save The Date
10. Baby Makes Three
11. Rivals
12. Perfect Gifts
13. Family First

Railers Volume 1 | *Railers Volume 2* | *Railers Volume 3* | *Railers Volume 4*

Owatonna U, College Hockey

Meet the men of Owatonna University's hockey team

Ryker (Owatonna U, 1)

Ryker is hockey royalty, Jacob is a poor country boy. Can two vastly different people find common ground and become the men they want to be?

Ryker comes from a long line of championship-winning hockey players. Playing college hockey to develop his game is his only focus, and nothing will stand in the way of him working to become the best player. He has no room for relationships, people who point out his flaws, or anyone who calls him on his dreams. He certainly has no place for love, and meeting Jacob is nothing but a useful distraction on the side. After all trying to get his Owatonna Eagles teammate into bed is less work and more play. When tragedy rocks his family, his charmed life crumbles, and the only person he can turn to is the same one who claims to hate him.

Jacob Benson has only known hard work and stifling conservative values his whole life. Born and raised in the small rural community of Eden Crossing, Minnesota, he's the only son of a hard-working but struggling dairy farming family. Jacob is using his skills in hockey to finance his way to an agricultural science degree. These four years at Owatonna U. will probably be the only time he has to enjoy life, gain acceptance about his sexuality, and live openly before his inevitable return to the farm. Running into a pretty rich boy like Ryker Madsen is putting a damper on his enjoyment of life away from home. Ryker's flip, conceited, carefree attitude grates on Jacob's every nerve. So why, if Ryker is everything he dislikes, does he want nothing more than to explore the sinful dreams that his annoying teammate stars in every night?

Ryker

———

Owatonna U Hockey (Hockey Romance)

1. Ryker
2. Scott
3. Benoit
4. Christmas Lights
5. Valentine's Hearts
6. Desert Dreams

Arizona Raptors

Coast to Coast (Arizona Raptors 1)

Coast To Coast

When opposites attract, this bottom-of-the-league team will never be the same again.

A stipulation in his father's will forces Mark back into the arms of a family that disowned him and leaves him one-third owner of a hockey team facing financial ruin. He doesn't even watch hockey, let alone like it, and wants nothing more than to head back to New York. Then there's the new coach, a stubborn, opinionated, irritating man with superiority issues and questionable music taste. Butting heads with Rowen becomes the new normal, but it comes with passionate debate and an all-consuming lust.

Challenged to rebuild one of the worst teams in the league into a future cup contender, Rowen can't pass up the opportunity. Never in his twenty years of hockey has he ever seen a team managed so badly or coached players overflowing with resentment and bigotry. Yet there's something about this team and this city that compels him to roll up his sleeves and start dismantling. If only Mark, one of three siblings who now own the Raptors, wasn't so damned rock-headed yet so damned appealing his job might be easier. It doesn't look like either is willing to give in, but one night in a dark, desert hotel changes everything.

Coast To Coast

Arizona Raptors (Hockey Romance)

1. Coast To Coast
2. Across the Pond
3. Shadow and Light
4. Sugar and Ice
5. School and Rock

Boston Rebels

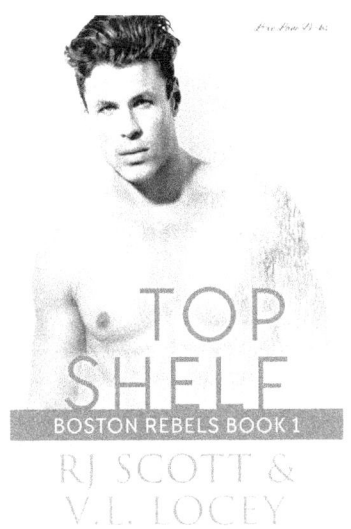

Top Shelf (Boston Rebels 1)

Acting on the attraction to his best friend's brother has always been off the table for Xander until a passionate hookup with Mason at a beach resort begins a love affair that burns long after summer ends.

Mason specializes in assisting same-sex couples on their journey to becoming parents and fighting every rule that blocks his way in the stuck-in-the-past agency that hired him. Living in his brother's pool house is rent-free, and every cent he earns he saves for his dream—that one day he'd have his own company helping others. The downside is that he has to see his annoying brother every day, the upside is that his brother's teammates from the

Boston Rebels make regular visits. The eye candy that passes Mason's window is almost enough to make him consider dating a hockey player, but not just any player though. Ever since Xander —his brother's childhood friend—came out as gay at a press conference, Mason's puppy love has turned into a burning attraction he can no longer ignore.

Hockey has been one of Xander's main focuses since he was old enough to balance on skates. Well, hockey and Mason Kingsley, but Mason was always unattainable. Now that he's about to see thirty candles on his birthday cake and is no longer hiding the fact he's gay, he's ready to find a soul mate to make his life complete. A summer vacation is just what he needs to have time to think, but when the Boston Rebels arriving in paradise with Mason in tow, thinking is the last thing he needs. One torrid night under a balmy moon and rules about not messing with his best friend's brother vanish on a warm, tropical breeze.

Summer romances don't generally last past Labor Day, but with the new season about to begin Xander and Mason are going to have to face the world and decide if their love is real enough to withstand everything.

Boston Rebels

Lost In Boston (Free Prequel Novella)

1. Top Shelf
2. Back Check
3. Snowed
4. Royal Lines
5. Blade
6. Rental

Chesterford Coyotes, Young Adult Romance

Off The Ice (Chesterford Coyotes, 1)

Off The Ice

A coming-of-age love story with high school, hockey rivalry, friendship, family, and coming out.

Soren's life changes in an instant when he and his younger brother are adopted by hockey royalty. Making sense of his new life is hard enough, but when he's enrolled in a private school it means facing a whole new set of problems. Navigating friendship, family, and hockey is one thing, but being attracted to the boy who vexes him is a whole new thing.

Felix has a reputation to protect. He's the kid who seems to have everything but looks can be deceiving. Spinning lies about his perfect life, he's created a fantasy world that even he has started to believe. Only, it's not long before everything crumbles, all of his pretty lies are revealed, and only his closest rival sees through his pain and stands by him.

Fighting is easy, friendship is hard, but love is everything.

Off The Ice

Chesterford Coyotes

1. Off The Ice
2. On Thin Ice
3. *Dance on Ice*

Free Reads

Please note - in all of these free stories, there will be some spoilers for the main series books.

Railers Short Stories

Volume 1 | Volume 2

LA Storm

Sparkle

The Colts - AHL Short Stories

Pucks & Percentages

Breakaway

Making the Save

Standalone

Waiting for Christmas

Also By RJ Scott

For a full list of ebooks and links please scan the code above or visit rjscott.co.uk/rjbooks

Meet RJ Scott

RJ writes MM romance—sometimes sweet, sometimes dark, always with a generous splash of angst and a hint of hurt/comfort.

A born romantic, she's convinced love is love—and every man deserves his happily ever after (especially the ones who swear they don't).

Website - gayromance.co.uk
Newsletter - gayromance.co.uk/mailing-list

Scan for a complete list of ebooks and links.

instagram.com/rjscott_author
amazon.com/author/rj-scott
bookbub.com/authors/rj-scott

Also By VL Locey

For a full list of ebooks and links please scan the code above or visit vllocey.com/stories-from-vl-locey

Meet V.L. Locey

V.L. Locey loves worn jeans, yoga, belly laughs, walking, reading and writing lusty tales, Greek mythology, the New York Rangers, comic books, and coffee. (Not necessarily in that order.)

She shares her life with her husband, her daughter, one dog, two cats, a flock of assorted domestic fowl, and two Jersey steers.

When not writing spicy romances, she enjoys spending her day with her menagerie in the rolling hills of Pennsylvania with a cup of fresh java in hand.

vllocey.com | vicki@vllocey.com
Newsletter - vllocey.com/newsletter

Scan for a complete list of ebooks and links.

facebook.com/V.L.Locey

x.com/vllocey

instagram.com/vl_locey

bookbub.com/authors/v-l-locey

goodreads.com/vllocey

pinterest.com/vllocey